Th
House, Holyhead

by

R. M. CARTMEL

Inspired by the 1942 film 'Casablanca'

Published by City Fiction

Copyright © 2019 R. M. Cartmel

ISBN: 978-1-910040-26-3

THE WHITE HOUSE

The year is 2039 and the United Kingdom is a distant memory. Scotland achieved its dream of independence and the European Union (the 'EU') welcomed them back. Ireland (and Northern Ireland) held a referendum and, by a large majority, united: there was a little pointless bloodshed, but power passed to Dublin. They were already members of the EU.

British politics (meaning England and Wales) disintegrated as the Conservatives were never forgiven by the populus for their betrayal over Brexit. Labour's period in minority government, following its period of vacillation, led to a financial crisis as they borrowed and borrowed and wrecked the once vibrant economy. New, smaller political parties were created and government became a matter of coalitions.

As time moved on, global warming became an ever-worrying challenge. The sea level was rising, despite the profusion of windmills and solar panels proliferating especially in Wales and East Anglia. A sea wall was built around London. Throughout the world, aeroplanes were phased out in favour of huge nuclear fusion powered airships whose waste product, the inert gas helium, was reused to fill their gasbags. Electric helicopters filled the skies, lifting passengers and cargo from the ground up to the giant airships.

Pods, as electric runabouts became known,

1

appeared everywhere followed by similarly powered vans and buses.

However, political strife was never far away and after a number of years of Westminster inertia, in 2029, Anglia took global warming seriously and declared independence. It did not help that Yarmouth, Wisbech, Holbeach and Harwich were now under water. Anglia developed a pyramid meritocracy allowing all to vote in local elections so creating an Anglian National Government, jokingly nicknamed all over the Island an 'Academic junta'. Its leader was called the 'senior lecturer'.

Wales already was ready for independence and rose up, painlessly. There was rejoicing in the hills and valleys. The West Country followed, renaming itself Wessex, and, modelling itself on the Anglian system, set up its Witan in Winchester.

For nearly ten years all went to plan. Anglia, Wales and Wessex started to negotiate firstly with Scotland, then Ireland and finally with the EU asking to re-join the now totally federalist movement.

In 2038 England created an army out of its fractious unemployed and invaded Anglia. Tensions developed elsewhere but England was hindered by its dire financial situation. The politicians were, however, desperate to maintain its borders including some control over its immediate island neighbours.

Holyhead, off the western coast of Anglesey on a small island of its own called Holy Island, is a small port where ferries ply the waters between North Wales and Dublin in Ireland. It has, however, been made very clear by their English 'advisors' that the only passengers on those ferries should have Welsh or European passports. Even the English passports must have a Welsh or Irish visa attached. That is unless they have a special pass issued by what the English still insist on calling the British Government. One source of Welsh travel visas is the police headquarters in Holyhead, and holders of English passports have to have persuasive reasons to liberate one of those precious Welsh visas.

These restrictions haven't stopped refugees in their thousands making for Holyhead in the hope of finding a way onto a ferry to Ireland, and from there, to catch an Airship to America or Europe. However getting a Welsh or Irish pass is extremely expensive or extremely difficult or both. And if you don't have the money or influence, all that is left for you is to sit in Holyhead, and wait, and wait, and wait.

§§§§

G'day. I'm Shane, and I'm from God's own Country, down under. So what, I hear you cry, is a true blue Aussie doing, running a bar on the edge of North Wales? Not an unreasonable question, which you might be able to work out yourself from what I've already told you. "I'm Shane" should have given you a big clue. An even bigger clue is to tell you that it was the name my parents gave me when I was born; I haven't relabelled myself in any way. Yes, you've got it; both my parents were cricket mad drongos. Shane has always been a good name for an Aussie cricketer to wear; we've had a Shane Warne, who was the best leg spinner the world has ever seen. Then there was Shane Lee, who played Shield cricket, and whose brother Brett was an internationally swift bowler, and finally there was Shane Watson who opened the batting in a baggy green cap for a while. I don't think my parentals would have minded what I did with my life long term, as long as it included playing cricket for Australia.

The problem was that while I do enjoy playing cricket, it rapidly became clear that, contrary to popular belief, you do need something else apart from a cricket name to be a great cricketer; you need a thing called talent. I know Colin Cowdrey's parents might tell you differently, and that he became a great player because of the initials they gave him at birth, but I reckon the old pommie batter was a good player because he knew which end to hold a bat. There must be so many others who have given their kids strange initials like SCG, in the hope of them playing for Australia at the Sydney Cricket Ground, and nobody ever heard of them again. As I was saying, to create a successful career in cricket, you need ability, but the talent gods passed me by. Mind you, I was found to be quite clever at other stuff and so I went to University in Adelaide. My parents were still disappointed in me. I didn't get into any college teams at any level, but I did earn a half decent degree, and, on the back of that, I was offered a place to do a Masters in Cambridge in England. Well the old dears were really thrilled by that, so I really didn't have any choice in the matter. Even if I had wanted to stay in Oz, I was on my way to the heart of England quicker than any Lillian Thomson bouncer. I was going to do a Masters in European History, but as far as my parentals were concerned, I was going there to learn how to bowl a proper Bosie like Benaud and get the pommie batters in a tangle at Lord's.

It's a strange thing looking at it, how cricket has

blithely refused to accept any of the changes that have happened to the old country recently. Despite it having voted to have a Brexit, and effectively blowing itself to pieces as a result; the island still gets to put out an 'English' Championship from which it selects an 'England' team, which includes Somerset players from Independent Wessex, Glamorgan players from Powys in Wales, and even Essex players from an Anglia which is currently under military rule from Westminster. They still play the odd test as well as the usual high-speed stuff. After all, Great Britain may be a single island but it is currently made up of five fiercely independent little countries, so I suppose it's a bit like the West Indies, all those funny little islands that don't seem to talk to each other much, and yet clubbing together to form one "national" team.

And of course, being in Cambridge, I was right in the middle of it when the balloon went up. Walking into Anglia was easy for the English army, especially as there wasn't much resistance to speak of. At the same time they hoped to discourage any other province who might be watching from a cautious distance thinking how much better the small independent countries were doing without any interference from Westminster. They were probably fairly twitchy about the Ridings of Yorkshire declaring independence. If it did, and decided that it also wanted an independent cricket team as well, like Pakistan when it separated from India in '48, the Poms would be completely up the creek. The last thing Westminster wanted from those other provinces was a movement of their own planning their own exit.

Somehow for me, staying in Anglia really wasn't an

option. I'm not going to go into details right now. Suffice it to say, I had about twenty-four hours notice to get out of Cambridge before the tanks arrived. A chum of mine from Cambridge called Ali and I caught a silly o'clock in the morning train to Birmingham, from where we caught a rather slower train that seemed to stop at every station from there to Shrewsbury, hoping that people weren't already on the lookout for me. But the stations remained deserted. Once we were in Shrewsbury however, it was easy enough to cross the border into Wales, where we rented a pod. Even if the Welsh were aware at that point what was going on the other side of the island, they certainly didn't seem interested in an Australian and an Asian tourist doing a spot of rock climbing in Wales. So Ali and I pottered along the coast road to the Menai Bridge and on into Anglesey, and from there along the road to Holyhead. The main road into Holyhead is so impressive I didn't immediately spot that it was a bridge onto another Island. Once in Holyhead, we stopped for a night in a friendly little gastro-pub called The White House to get our bearings, and find out what exactly we needed to do to get passes to get over the water to Ireland. The answer was 'lots,' and it was going to cost a load more than I had ever owned in my life, so we had to find jobs, and start saving up.

The White House was a bit short staffed, at that point in time, as the Polish couple that ran the kitchen had up-sticks and left on the boat for Dublin as soon as any sign of trouble started. I stayed on to help out, and to give myself a little time to get earning the money needed to bribe the appropriate person to get that pass. To cut a long story short, it's a year later, and I now just about run the place. I'm told locals even call us 'Shane's Aussie Eatery,' which is a bit daft, as I haven't seen a 'roo' steak anywhere in my time on the Big Island. But I guess we get by.

Ali and I had first met in a pub in Cambridge where I used to hang out when I wasn't working on my dissertation. I guess we got to know each other pretty well over time. He was the pub's house musician, playing god knows how many different instruments, and when the balloon went up, it appeared he needed to get out of Cambridge in a hurry as well; I never did ask why. If he ever feels one day I need to know, I'm sure he'll tell me, and I might tell him my story in return.

We took on the kitchens, which started as a ping and ding. You know, take it out the freezer, bung it in the nuke, press 'ping' and five minutes later 'ding' you've got something warm to swallow with your pint. Ali did potwash to start with, but I knew what he really wanted to do was get behind that tatty ancient piano in the bar, or even get out his old guitar, and sing the blues a bit. As I took over, I guess I changed the place. I found a couple of welsh speakers who could really cook mutton and leeks from the ground upwards, while I became the face of the place. Ali and I even turned out in the occasional cricket match. Neither of us was anywhere near as good as the locals, but our team presented this Asian feller and me as if we were their international stars. Ali used to toss the ball high in the air, and when it didn't spin he would grin, knowingly at the batter up the other end. Used to worry the wombats out of the opposition and it usually took them a little while to work out exactly how good we really weren't.

§§§§§

Joey McGregor was more weasel than man. I know he had a Scottish name, but he didn't resemble any Scot that I've ever met. He was forever coming to me with some little knick-knack, which I suspected he had effectively stolen from someone waiting just outside the docks, willing to sell any possession, even their bodies, to find the money to get one of those elusive passes to Ireland. He would bring whatever he had got and ask me to look after it for a few days. He was at least true to his word in that sense, as he never left his trivia very long in my place, and he always came by with an 'I've found a buyer' and he would often leave me a bit of cash for my trouble. You just know that it's an under the counter sort of business, the way that cash is still used in Holyhead. Cash is so much more anonymous than the electronic money you wear on your wrist. You know, wristies are funny things; back in my father's day, Dad wore a device on his wrist that told him what time it was, period. These things we call wristies are rather smaller than his old watch, but carry my identity 'papers', access to various bank accounts, access to services like summoning a pod if I needed one anywhere on the Big Island, and it still tells the time. The device probably tells the powers that be where I am too, so that's why everyone's so cautious about when they use them, and when they still use cash. There was never anything trustworthy about doing deals with the Poms, there never has been.

Why did people like Joey go about involving me in their business? To be honest I don't really care. The place is teeming with Welsh Police and English soldiers, but then when they're in my place, they all seem to be off duty, and sometimes they even ask me to store some booty for them as well. Okay, I can cope with that, it's none of my business. I'm neutral, I don't rattle their cages, and they don't rattle mine. I suppose that's what they mean by 'hiding stuff in plain sight.'

'Shane, can I leave something with you for a few days?' was his usual opening gambit.

'Aren't you running out of little old ladies to prey on?' was my usual contemptuous reply. It was no different this time.

'I think you're going to be impressed with me this time.' That was a change; Joey knew he never impressed me. He reached into his inner jacket pocket and pulled out an envelope. It was the wrong sort of envelope to be carrying money, and wasn't thick enough to be carrying a lot of it anyway.

'So what is it this time?'

'They're English Royal Travel Documents,' he said proudly.

That was different anyway. He'd nicked some rare souvenirs from his little old victim this time. They might be quite valuable to a collector if he could find the right one. 'Okay,' I said, 'I am a little more impressed, I'll give you that. Just don't leave them here too long. If there's a hue and cry about the theft, I'll burn them.'

'Oh, don't worry about that, Shane, I already have a bidding war about these. I'm afraid that they will be stolen off me if I'm found walking about with them. A couple of days, top whack.' He passed me the envelope, and walked out of the room.

I have a number of secret places in my office, including a couple of safes. I chose the safe where I keep the booty where I store the stuff the English soldiers have left for my safe keeping, and tossed it in there behind the silver menorah, which had surely been 'borrowed' from a synagogue, somewhere. I was kind of hoping that once this was all over, I might return the menorah to the place where it belonged. I'm not the slightest bit religious, but I know some people are, and it upsets them when their religious artefacts get stolen. I can remember watching a whole download once about some invading army nicking the Arc of the Covenant. It was a great bit of hokum.

I shut the safe and locked it.

I walked out of my office out into the bar. Ali stopped playing whatever it was he was playing, and started on something else completely. 'Were you playing it?' I asked as I strode in his direction.

'Of course I wasn't,' he replied awkwardly. Ali had one real difficulty with me, he couldn't tell a lie convincingly.

I looked down my nose at him. I didn't need to say anything.

'Oh okay, I was, but why is that so wrong?'

'Its taboo in here,' I snarled. Most people would have shut up at that, but I guess Ali knew me too well to be intimidated.

'But why? I like it, and back in Cambridge it was your favourite number.'

'Back in Cambridge, it was *her* favourite number, and I never want to hear it again.' I turned on my heels, at least half looking for someone else I might mistake for the woman from Cambridge, that happened often enough, but she wasn't here today. Instead I came face-to-face with the local Police Chief. I have usually found Rhys Evans to be an amiable man, but then I didn't have to do business with him; not yet anyway. I supposed that when the time came and I did end up doing business with him on my own behalf, it would be to my own benefit if we understood each other in advance. We certainly knew that there are things that each of us doesn't want the other to know and, like sensible men, we avoid those subjects.

'Fancy a drink?' he said, 'I'm buying.'

Evans? Putting his hand in his own pocket? We both knew that when his bar tab gets too high, I give him a bill. He then looks me right in the eye, and tears the bill up and we both smile. I think we know that one day in the future I will collect on that debt. However, if he was going to pour something expensive down my throat, I think I wanted his contribution up front. We walked over to the bar. Behind the bar Myfanwy James was serving; pretty girl, nice eyes, and a good set of pipes when she gets up to sing on a busy night. We all call her Miff for short, 'I'll have what he's having,' Evans said.

'Do you really want a glass of water?' Miff asked with the slightly coy smile that would probably get her in a lot of trouble if it wasn't widely known that she was one of my employees. I think some people think she and I have a thing going.

Evans looked quizzically at me, 'You mean it's really true that you don't drink with customers?'

'It really is,' I replied.

'On this occasion, I think you ought to change your mind,' he replied, quite firmly.

This was becoming interesting. I raised an eyebrow and told Miff, 'I'll have what he usually has.'

'Do you want it in a glass, or would you like the whole bottle?' she asked.

What on earth does Evans drink? I wondered. 'There's a table over there,' she said, 'I'll get Paul to bring it over to you.' She pointed at an empty booth along one wall. It was early in the evening, and the place hadn't really started to fill up yet. And yes he pointed his wristy at her reader, and paid whatever it was worth on the spot.

'So what's this all about then?' I asked as we were both sitting in the booth.

'What do you know about Andrew Ryan?'

'He's the most wanted man on the whole of the Island. The locals call him the head of the Resistance, the English just call him a terrorist. It depends whose side you're on.' I replied dryly.

'And which side are you on, Shane?' he asked gently, but his eyes flickered with interest. We both knew that I had just been asked the most important question I had been asked since I left Cambridge.

'Neither,' I replied, 'This bar is the most neutral place on the whole of the Big Island, and I intend to keep it that way. Look,' I waved a hand at the bar that was still far from full. There were a few locals in one corner, a few English soldiers in another corner, and coming towards us was a little old man carrying a tray with a bottle and two glasses on it. I remarked to Evans as he got there, 'You come in here, you drink, you have fun, and you leave your civil war outside on the street.' The bottle was put on the table. It had a screw cap like many wine bottles do nowadays, but I was seriously impressed with the one he had chosen. Maybe it wasn't desperately expensive as wine goes, but a red German Dornfelder from Boppard is difficult enough to find anywhere in Britain at the moment, and I was aware that the previous owner of

12

the bar had acquired our current stock by finagling a complex deal which involved several strange people in Dublin, Cork and Cherbourg.

'Your very good health,' he toasted me.

'Chug-a-Lug,' I replied and we both drank. I was quite impressed, the wine had indeed aged quite well in our little beer cellar. I looked up at him, and asked, 'you were going to tell me something about this Ryan bloke,' I said.

He nodded, 'Well he caused all sorts of trouble in Anglia after the invasion.'

'For which they executed him,' I replied, finishing his story; I thought.

'It appears that they didn't,' Evans replied, 'they only said they did.'

'Really? I heard it said the bastard was slippery, but I had no idea he was that slippery. So what does the Anglian eel have to do with us out here?'

'His last reported sighting was in Chepstow, a few days ago,' he began.

'He's in Wales?'

'He is, and they say he's heading for Ireland. If that's true, he's either going to Haverford West, or he's coming here, and if he wants to get to Dublin Airport to catch an airship,' he continued slowing down, expecting me to complete the sentence.

'He'd come here,' I duly did.

'Exactly. Now there's something else, a courier was knocked off his motorbike near Bangor yesterday, and his bag was stolen.'

'Go on,' I said. This was becoming more interesting by the minute.

'He was carrying among other things, two English Royal passes to Ireland. I'm not sure I believe in that sort of coincidence.'

'Why would he need two passes? Has he put on weight or something?'

Evans looked at me, 'No, He's travelling with a woman, and rumour has it that she's very good-looking.'

'You look impressed Rhys,' I replied.

'To be honest, I am. I'm getting a lot of pressure from the English to the tune that Ryan must not get out of Wales. Nobody would dare being found with those documents on their person. The English can be quite ruthless about these things, even on Welsh soil. So they have to have been hidden somewhere. And the fact that the courier was killed in Bangor, makes Holyhead the most likely place they will be hiding.'

'Killed?' I asked, with a sense of foreboding. Joey McGregor had been right a few minutes ago. I was becoming more impressed by the minute.

'Oh yes, there was a length of wire stretched across the road, I'm told. The pathologist said it took his head clean off. Anyway Shane, that's all I have to say. I'm supposed to be keeping a close eye on you.'

'I hope you'll be keeping your other eye on our old friend Tubba down at the Green Shamrock as well,' I replied.

'We have police watching the Shamrock too.'

I think I needed to have eyes at the back of my head sometimes, there seemed to be some sort of kerfuffle going on by the bar. 'Excuse me,' I said, and got up and walked over.

There was an English soldier with his paws all over Miff, and she obviously wasn't enjoying the experience. Mind you she had a large glass of something interestingly coloured in the hand that wasn't exactly fighting the soldier off as such, so perhaps he was feeling he had already paid for what he was claiming.

'I'm afraid I don't allow people to manhandle the staff,' I said fairly gently, in the hope that he would understand what I was saying without making an issue out of it. We shared momentary eye contact, and he backed down. However I did feel that that wasn't going to be the end of it.

'My hero,' slurred Miff as she slung both her arms round my neck. Her breath smelled inflammable. What was in that mixture? I must make a note that bar staff will not mix Mickey Finns to be drunk by other bar staff.

'I think it's about time you went home to bed,' I said fairly gently.

'Can I stay with you again tonight?'

'Not tonight, kiddo,' I replied. On the one side was that foxy little body that had been most enjoyable on occasions. On the other side there was that breath, and the distinct possibility of her throwing up all over me during the night. I looked around for Paul. 'Can you get her a taxi home, and pour her into it?' I asked him.

'Sure thing Boss,' the old Pole replied, 'come along honey,' he said to her. 'You'll feel much better in the morning.'

She let him guide her out, but as she went through the door she howled despairingly at me, 'But we love each other.' I ignored her.

I watched the English soldier to make sure he wasn't going to follow them out, but he wasn't. He was already engaged in conversation with a group of soldiers dealing a pack of cards.

I went back to my table with Evans who had been watching the whole incident with interest. 'You're a very generous soul, Shane,' he said. 'I can't think of many men who would have turned an offer like that down.'

I looked at him without saying anything. There wasn't any point. I knew how Evans's mind worked, certainly as far as the female of the species was concerned, and it wasn't going to be worth my while to openly disagree with him. I took another mouthful from the contents of my glass.

We have a quasi-legal casino in the back of the bar. They play Roulette, a little Baccarat, a few craps, you know the sort of low skill stuff which gives the bar a slight edge. Evans lets us get away with it provided he's allowed to occasionally frequent it, and win a little. He probably has quite a reasonable second income if you add up all the bars in Holyhead all allowing him to 'win a little' in their back room casinos. I'm not quite sure what the actual law states, but then I'm not stupid enough to ask. Raoul is a Frenchman we took on to run the casino to give it a bit of that Monte Carlo glitz, though I suspect he comes from a part of France that is nearer to Holyhead than it is to Monte Carlo. He has this skill of not being anywhere in sight, and suddenly being right there at your elbow.

'Boss,' he said apologetically, 'It won't happen again, but we've had a winner, Boss, and he wants the money in cash.'

I asked him how much, and he told me. Well, Raoul was right, we don't carry twenty thousand Euros at the tables, it's asking to be robbed. We don't have that sort of cash in Welsh pounds either, but people tend not to gamble in Welsh, as we don't exchange currency at the bar. The exchange rates are too unstable. I nodded at Evans, 'Stay there a moment Rhys, I've just got to go and sort this out.' I walked up the stairs into my office. I suppose it was really the front room of my flat over the business, with a kitchen, an ablution department and a bedroom off it. But in reality I saw the whole bar as my living area. I walked over to the smaller less obvious safe and let myself into it. I took out the pistol, and slipped it into my jacket pocket, there was no point in my being mugged for carrying that sort of money, even for a few yards. That sort of money could get you out of urban Holyhead and planted in patches of newly created swamp where they'd never find you again, if you weren't very careful. I took out the pile of cash I kept for just this purpose, and peeled off twenty thousand. I put the rest back. Not to worry, we'd replenish the stock over the coming days.

I slipped the cash into an envelope and stuck it into the inner pocket of my jacket, closed the safe and spun the wheel. I cast an eye around as I walked to the door, switched off the lights, and set off back down the stairs. I walked straight through to the casino where Raoul was talking to a tall thin man who was not disguising his impatience very well.

'Congratulations sir,' I said shaking his hand with the envelope. 'You've been very lucky. I don't suppose we'll see you again.'

He shook his head, and I added, 'best of luck with the rest of your life.' The man scuttled out indecently quickly with his hand in his pocket, presumably still holding my envelope.

17

I went back to the bar to re-join Evans. He was looking at his wristy. Presumably he was checking the time. 'I must go soon,' he said, 'something's coming up.' I couldn't imagine what that could be. Could it have anything to do with a man walking swiftly out of my bar with his hand in his pocket? More than likely.

§§§§§

He hadn't even reached the door when four figures in bottle green uniforms walked in. They came in adopting a 'missing man' formation, and it was obvious who the leader was. He had scrambled eggs on the peak of his cap and far heavier epaulettes than the others. He also had that air about him. Evans twitched, almost as if he was about to bow, and then caught himself in the nick of time. 'Colonel,' he said, and turned on his heels, and hurried back into the bar. He found Paul, and grabbed him by the shoulder.

'Paul,' he said urgently. 'Colonel Willoughby's here. Can you get him the best seat in the house?'

Paul gave him a beatific smile, 'I've already arranged it, knowing he would take it anyway.' He waved at a table in the corner facing into the room, with the backs of all its chairs facing to the wall. The Colonel and his entourage were already sitting down at it.

Evans nodded at them. 'Can you get them a bottle of Champagne and some glasses?' he told Paul.

Paul bustled off, and the policeman walked over to the Colonel's table. 'Colonel, I've ordered you a bottle of Champagne, on the house, and I've laid on a little entertainment for you this evening.'

'On the house?'

'The Landlord and I have, shall I say, a little understanding.'

The Colonel smiled knowingly and went on, 'and the entertainment?'

'Oh yes, I've arranged for the man who killed your courier to be arrested here in this bar this evening.'

'I would expect nothing less,' he replied acidly, as Paul arrived with a tray carrying an obviously cold glistening bottle of Champagne and some glasses. The waiter picked up the bottle, and put his hand round the cork and with a deft twisting movement, noiselessly removed it.

'We don't want to attract unwanted attention, or to waste any of the nectar,' Paul said to the surrounding English. 'We have not just won a motor race or launched a ship.' You could tell the English were not amused by his Polish accent, which got much more Polish in the presence of soldiers in uniform.

'Quite,' said the Colonel accepting the first glass.

Paul had only just left the table and its occupants had hardly started talking among themselves, when it all started to go down. I did tell you the excitement never stops at The White House, didn't I? Joey McGregor was at the till buying some gambling chips, when he felt a huge paw grab his left shoulder, and a voice snarling in his ear that he was under arrest, or some such platitude. McGregor was a wriggly weasel, and he wriggled out of the officer's grip. The next moment he was trying to hide behind me. 'Shane, you've got to help me.' he wheedled up at me.

I looked down my nose at McGregor, 'I haven't "got" to do anything,' I replied, 'you have to sell it to me, just like everyone else. What's going on?'

'They're going to arrest me,' he said.

19

I stepped smartly to my left, leaving him in full view of the Welsh policeman, and a huge English Army sergeant. 'As I was saying, boyo,' said the policeman, 'you're under arrest.'

'Shane,' McGregor positively squealed.

The Sergeant looked at me, and I shrugged, as if to say, 'Nothing to do with me.'

They manhandled McGregor to the main entrance of the bar, and as they opened the front door, McGregor whirled round with a pistol in his hand and fired without aiming, behind him and rushed out. The huge Englishman swore, and grabbed his left arm. The Welshman turned and looked at his colleague for a moment, and then rushed off out after McGregor. I patted my jacket just checking that McGregor hadn't picked my pocket and taken my pistol a few moments before, but it was still there. A moment or so later, you could hear a fusillade of shots from the outside.

I raised my voice. 'It's all over, nothing to worry about. Carry on enjoying yourselves.' However I was aware that there was something to worry about, and I made my way back up to the office. My pistol needed to be not in my pocket any longer, and that envelope had to be someplace safer than the British Booty safe, though, for the moment I couldn't think of one. I opened the safe, put my pistol in it, and got the envelope out, and sat down at my desk and thought about it.

Meanwhile, what was going on next down in the bar, Paul told me about later. The front door opened and in walked a couple. The man caught Paul's eye, obviously the correct eye to catch, as there was no-one else wandering around with a tea towel over his left arm. 'I have a table booked,' said the man to Paul, and he continued, 'ideally as far away from the English Army as possible.'

'The name?' Paul asked.

'Andrew Ryan,' he replied.

'This way,' said Paul, and led them away from the area that was beginning to fill up with increasingly boisterous men in uniforms of varying persuasions. As they walked to their table, Ali and the woman's eyes met, and there was a flash of recognition between them. As the two sat down, Ryan ordered drinks for the pair of them.

'Darling,' she said, 'I think we ought to go. I have a definitely uneasy feeling about this place.'

'Nonsense,' he replied. 'It looks a delightful place. It's absolutely teeming with the English, and they only go to the best places.'

'Yes, but they're the English.'

'You worry too much, the English can't do a damn thing to me in Wales. This isn't an occupied country, they're simply here as advisors. And besides,' he paused, 'I arranged to meet Joey McGregor here in The White House.'

'What does he look like?'

'I haven't the faintest idea, I've never met him. But he will know me, my picture's everywhere.'

'You two look you might be heading to Ireland,' said a voice with an Irish lilt behind Ryan's shoulder. 'Can I be of assistance?'

'Joey McGregor?' Ryan asked.

'Er no,' replied the man, but he sat down anyway. 'The unfortunate Mr. McGregor got himself arrested a little while ago.'

'So what do we do now?' asked the woman.

'Can I borrow you for a moment,' the man said to

Ryan, 'It may not be a complete disaster, well, not for you anyway. Though I wouldn't be holding out a lot of hope for poor Joey McGregor himself.' The man gave an official looking pass with a green cover to Ryan.

Ryan flipped through it and gave it back, 'That isn't a lot of use to me,' he said, it's got your picture in it, and we don't look anything like each other.'

'Just establishing my credentials,' the Irishman replied, 'Mickey Riley at your service. If you wouldn't mind hanging on here,' he said to the woman, 'I would recommend you enjoy the music for a moment. The musician over there has quite a reputation round here. Ryan followed Riley off to a corner where there were various other people sitting in a huddle. She looked back at Ali, then got up and walked over to him.

'Hello Ali,' she said, 'Long time no see.'

'What are you doing here, Jenny? Please make yourself scarce before he sees you. You're bad news as far as Shane's concerned.'

'Is he here?'

Ali paused and looked awkward. 'No, he went home,' he said after a moment.

'When will he be back?'

'Probably tomorrow, but we don't know so much nowadays. Umm, he's got a girlfriend over at the Green Shamrock, you see, and they say she's quite hot, so sometimes we don't see him for days at a time.'

Jenny looked at him gently. He could tell already that she didn't believe a word that he'd said. 'Play it Ali,' she said.

'What?'

'Play Layla, Ali.'

'Don't know if I can remember it, Jenny.'

'Nobody who worked out an arrangement of a song that originally involved two lead guitars and a bass for a single piano would ever forget it. It wasn't just Eric Clapton's masterpiece, it was yours too. Play it Ali.'

Ali turned round and played that rolling opening on the piano and went into the song itself. He didn't often sing the words, they weren't that important, just the melody.

Up in my study, I was aware there was something going on down in the bar, and, pushing the envelope into my jacket breast pocket, I got up and went to the door. When I got as far as the landing, I knew exactly what was going on, Ali was playing that bloody tune. I was down those stairs in a flash. 'Ali, I thought I told you, never to play that,…' He'd stopped playing already as he was aware I was heading his way like a charging rhino. However he wasn't looking at me, but somewhere to my left. I stopped and looked at where he was looking. He was gawping at someone else who looked like Jenny. Everywhere I look there are people who look like Jenny. I've seen pictures on billboards that look like Jenny. Damn it I've even seen zoo animals I had to look at twice to persuade myself they weren't Jenny. When I look again, of course I can tell that they're koalas or something, but seeing fake-Jenny Laings has become so much a part of my life, a trick my mind plays on me. I hated it, but it was something I'd got used to it since leaving Cambridge.

I looked back at Ali, and then back at the woman. Oh crap, it still looked like Jenny. She had the same lustrous raven hair. Funny, many Welsh women, and

Irish women for that matter, have black hair, but somehow theirs is a more matt black than hers. Jenny's is lustrous, and shiny, almost as if she'd put some product into it, which of course she never did. I knew, I had run my fingers through that hair often enough in Cambridge. It is naturally shiny, and if you get closer you could see they aren't coloured highlights, just lights. The same way as I knew what her shape was like inside those clothes, I had seen her naked often enough. I had held that body so close, I had even been inside that body. And here she was, what the hell was she doing in Holyhead?

'Play something soft,' I said to Ali, 'just not that.' And I walked over to her.

'Shane? Is that really you?'

I recognised that voice too. It really was her this time.

'Shane,' said a voice behind me. That one I recognised as belonging to Rhys Evans. 'May I introduce you to someone, who I think you may have heard of?'

I turned and there was a man possibly approaching middle age, but wearing a face that had obviously known many difficulties on its journey to Holyhead. 'This is Andrew Ryan.'

'One hears a lot about Shane in Holyhead,' said the man as he shook my hand.

'One hears a lot about Andrew Ryan everywhere,' I replied.

'They said he was travelling with a beautiful woman,' Evans continued, 'but I can see they were guilty of an outrageous understatement.' He paused to allow her to pretend to simper embarrassedly before he continued, 'this is Miss….'

'Jenny,' I replied, almost catching her eye.

'Shane,' she said, looking away.

'Oh,' said Evans, 'You two know each other.'

'Come and join us for a drink Mister Shane,' said Ryan.

'Shane never drinks with customers,' said the policeman apologetically.

'I'd be delighted,' I replied ignoring him completely.

'Well I never,' said Evans, 'This evening is full of surprises.'

We went back to Ryan's table and we sat down. Evans retrieved his bottle of Dornfelder, which still had a bit in the bottom, and he emptied it into a glass. I was just about to pour a splash of water into the Islay malt Paul had brought me together with a tiny jug of room temperature tap water. He knew how I liked to drink it if I was drinking to be pleasant company.

'Missster Ryan,' hissed a serpent like voice above and behind me.

Rhys Evans was up like he had sat on a hot coal. 'Colonel Willoughby, won't you join us?'

'Must he?' remarked Ryan drily. 'I would really not share air with a member of the English Army, if it's all the same to you, Inspector Evans.'

'It's Superintendent Evans,' Rhys replied, slightly stiffly.

'Really?' came out of both the Colonel and Ryan's mouths simultaneously with an equal amount of surprise. Under other circumstances they might both have laughed.

'This is a pleasure I have been waiting for a long time,' said the Colonel.

'May I say that the pleasure is all yours,' Ryan replied drily, 'Personally, it was one I would just has soon have done without.'

'I agree, this is neither the time nor the place for us to have the discussions that we need to have. May I suggest the Superintendent's office at nine o'clock tomorrow morning?'

'You can wait outside it if you like,' replied Evans, 'I'm normally expected in about ten. I would hate to unsettle my constables.'

'Ten o'clock it is then,' snapped the Colonel.

'Superintendent, I am under your jurisdiction here,' said Ryan, 'Is this your wish?'

'Take it as a polite request,' he replied. 'And do rest assured, you will be perfectly safe. Especially if you bring the exquisite Miss Laing with you.'

'We'll be there,' she replied, 'and we will have breakfasted, so you won't need to feed or water us at all.' There was an edge to her voice that I didn't remember from before.

'Good day,' said the Colonel standing up and saluting, 'till tomorrow.' He walked off, back to the group of men in green, chatting to Evans who was following him like an obedient puppy dog.

'I don't trust that man an inch,' Jenny remarked across me to Ryan.

'He's dressed in an English army uniform,' I said, perhaps to remind everyone I was still there. 'That level of trust's a no-brainer.'

'They really mean to get you this time,' Jenny said, ignoring me.

'Well I've been caught in London, Cambridge, and in Bristol, twice, but they haven't managed to hang on to me yet,' he replied with a grin.

'Ladies and Gentlemen,' said a rather stentorian voice into the microphone by Ali's piano. 'May I remind you that it's five minutes to closing time. Drink up please.'

'And at the moment we do have a curfew to enforce,' said Evans, returning to our table. 'I would hate to catch myself out after hours, and be forced to fine myself. I would find that one of the more difficult bills to tear up. May I recommend you return to your hotel?' That last remark he addressed to Ryan and Jenny.

They tossed back the last of their drinks and walked to the door. As they did, Jenny looked over and caught my eye, hers narrowing slightly. I had managed to avoid catching her eye up till that moment, but when it had finally happened, it was like a thousand volts of electricity passing through me. Then the couple was lost to view.

I walked through the throng as it made its way to the door. I made my way to the bar, where Paul was cashing up. 'Any more of that bottle of Ardbeg you gave me a shot of?' I asked.

'Water, Shane?' he asked.

'No thanks, just the bottle.

He passed it to me. I picked up a glass, and walked across to a table near the piano where Raoul was waiting with the evening's takings from the casino.

'I'm sorry Shane,' said Raoul, 'I haven't yet made up for the loss we had earlier.'

'Don't worry,' I replied, 'You will.' I put the takings in an envelope, and wrote *Casino* and the date on it, and added *minus twenty thousand from the safe*. 'See you tomorrow Shane,' said Raoul, and he joined the crowd squeezing through the door into the street.

I poured myself a scotch from the bottle, as Paul came up to me with the bar takings. They weren't cash takings, but dockets from peoples' wristies, which would need counting and checking against our machine. The Taxman would need to know all that, but at least the Taxman in Holyhead speaks English, not always the case in North Wales nowadays. The dockets also went into a brown envelope, on which I wrote, *Bar* and the date. I looked at the bottle, it was about half full, so I added on to the envelope *minus half a bottle of Ardbeg, but includes a contribution from Evans.*

'Good evening Shane,' said Paul and he headed for the door.

I took another couple of mouthfuls of whisky. I looked at Ali.

'Play it Ali,' I said.

'What?' he asked, as if he didn't know.

'Play Layla, if she can stand it, so can I.'

'Hadn't you best go up to bed now mate,' he said. 'You've got a lot of bureaucracy to do in the morning, to bring those accounts up to date.'

'Play it Ali. She's coming back.'

'How do you know that? Oh please, don't go there. She fucks with your head that woman. Go up to bed and forget about her.'

'Just you play that sodding piano,' I snarled, and refilled my glass.

He played Layla. He played Layla like he had never played it before, and when he got to the chorus, he sang, 'Layla, you've got me on my knees.'

I think when he got to the slower piano bit, I must have nodded off.

§§§§

Flashback; Cambridge the year before

The sight that greeted my eyes as I walked in was somewhat disconcerting, especially to a young man newly arrived from down under. The room was almost completely dark apart from the odd coloured light in the darkest of corners. Those bulbs were mainly red, and the whole ambience rather reminded me of certain streets of ill repute I had heard about in Sydney. There were little pockets of girls dancing together, out of self-protection round the pillars, and boys prowling the empty spaces between the pillars like wolves. I didn't know who looked more frightened, the girls or the boys. The only thing that was possible to do over that noise was to sign to a girl you were looking at if she wanted to dance.

"C'mon," said Will, my mate, standing by the door, where I could just about hear him, 'What do you think of those two?' he asked, and tugged at my sleeve. We took a deep breath and dived into the maelstrom. Before I had properly orientated myself, I had danced a slightly built raven-haired girl towards the bar, and Will had manoeuvred her companion in a similar direction. The door to the bar was open but the hubbub from the meat market, was reduced enough to allow some form of conversation. The bar was marginally better lit too, so having selected ones victim, it gave a girl, or a boy, the opportunity to see exactly the nature of the trophy that had been won in the darkness next door. Even in the market itself, I could see that the girl fate had selected for me was quite pretty. Under marginally better light, she was even prettier.

"Thank god we're out of that," said the girl whom Will had danced into the bar, "I was beginning to feel self-conscious."

"Really?" said the dark-haired girl, "I was really rather enjoying it."

"Drinks?" asked Will.

"Coke," said the girl Will had rescued from the Maelstrom, "Cinzano Bianco," said the one who'd followed me. I escorted them to a table, where they parked, and I went to help Will with the drinks. While we were collecting the drinks, we worked out between us which girl we were each going to try to charm. Disgraceful things young men aren't they? Will said he would like to talk to 'Coke', which left me with 'Cinzano', which suited me just fine. I liked the look of her dark hair and her smile. They obviously liked the look of us enough to stick around, as they were still at the table when we got back.

"I'm Jenny Laing," said the dark girl who drank Cinzano, "I'm studying English at Girton."

"And I'm Liz Powell," said the fair haired girl, "studying Philosophy and Psychology at the same place."

'Jennifer?' I asked.

'Genevieve, like the car,' Jenny replied.

We introduced ourselves too, in the same way, name rank and serial number; or in Cambridge's case, name, subject and college.

I was about to move the conversation on when Jenny beat me to it. 'I think this Fresher's Ball is such a good idea, don't you? Especially if you want to meet people, and at University, it's so important to meet people, don't you think?'

'Perhaps,' said Liz, 'but I was beginning to wonder what sort of people we were going to meet at a place like this. There were some nasty looking prowlers in there.'

'You're not necessarily out of the wood yet,' Will said and leered at her.

'What, sounding like you do?' asked Jenny, in a fairly accent free voice of her own. 'There is no way you could be the sort of animal Liz is after. She likes them rough and ready. So if you're rough, she's ready!'

'What!' spluttered Liz; I think it was an in-joke that Liz thought was still 'work in progress' between themselves, I don't think Liz was ready for it to be given a public performance quite yet. It was rather like the ramp-shot, there always has to be a first time when you try it out in a game. In my case, I had been quite lucky to hang on to my teeth.

From thereon in the conversation drifted into the usual pleasantries, who's your father, how's your mother, what did your brother die of, when did you last see your uncle, you know the sort of tedious thing, and all the time Jenny Laing laughed gaily, quite often at comments that really weren't in the least bit funny, flashing her brilliant blue eyes from beneath her wavy dark fringe. Her skin was lightly tanned, presumably from a summer in the sun. She didn't appear to be wearing much make up, on her face, but then again she could just have been better trained in its use, than I was in its detection. And yes, I could tell I was attracted to her. In fact I would go so far as to say that I couldn't take my eyes off her, even then. Was this what people talked about when they talked of love at first sight? Complete stuff and nonsense, of course, how could anyone fall in love with someone you don't even know?

Despite her initial excitement with the meat market, even Jenny tired off it fairly quickly, so we all went off to Will's room in college in a pod. Yes, the first thing I had done on arriving in Anglia, was make sure my Australian permit worked here, and I had got myself a pod pass tapped into my wristy.

Will produced a pot of really rather good coffee, and we settled down to try out a 'serious conversation'. But the conversation soon made its probably inevitable turn to one of the three 'forbiddens', sex, religion or politics. Politics, it was in our case, and Anglia's independence cropped up, and as far as I understood it, Jenny was in favour of it, the other two rather less so, Liz was quite emphatically in favour of re-unification at the next possible moment, with no obvious explanation on how that might be achieved.

The conversation eventually switched to lighter topics, and finally the girls announced they needed their beauty sleep, and Jenny summoned a pod of her own, but not until after we had all agreed to meet up on Parker's Piece the following day at two. It was only when I went to bed with a warm smiling feeling inside, that I realised I hadn't thought about Kylie all evening.

"Come in!" and in I went. Jenny was dressed, and how! "We're going to a party," she said, "There's one in Magdalen this evening, and I feel like waving a leg," and to demonstrate the point she waved a particularly lissom one at me.

I have to say that the idea of a dance rather appealed to me. I hadn't really seen Jenny dance before, despite the fact we had met at an event that was billed as a dance, but for one reason or another, we hadn't actually got round to dancing; and I was fascinated to see how she made out. The walk to Magdalen took us some twenty minutes during which we bored each other silly about how we had spent our first few academic days in Cambridge.

She had gone to a lecture by her professor and apparently it was as awful as his English, despite the fact it purported to be his subject. He had apparently delivered the whole lecture in Chaucerian English, complete with pronunciation. She had found it difficult to keep her eyes open, especially as her brother had kept her up talking well into the night. I wished I had been her brother; he seemed to be an all round good guy with whom she was willing to sit up talking for hours. Mind you if I had been, then my thoughts about how she looked in that little dark blue skirt would have been singularly inappropriate. He was articled at the Bar in London, and she assured me that we would all know his name in the future. As an aside, I hoped that it would not be for spending the night in his sister's room in Cambridge.

She was dressed in a light, fluffy, Oxford blue sweater, which followed the curves of her body at the same time making them look as if they were in soft focus, and moving south, that short skirt of contrasting midnight blue almost denim material. Her legs were sheathed in tights that made them look as if they had had good exposure to last summer's sun before they disappeared into her boots, which laced up to two thirds of the way up her shins. But the spectacular addition to her whole outfit was a thick black shiny patent leather belt, which, buckled loosely in front of her navel, just rested on her hips, leaving an obvious gap between the buckle and her fluffy sweater. Oh, and yes, one other thing, she could dance too. As she moved, her hair flew everywhere, and yet she appeared in complete control of it, so that at the end of each number, it was just exactly where she wanted it to be. And this spectacular young woman was here with me. I could not believe my good fortune. I had been in Cambridge for precisely one day, and I had met up with a goddess and we had made contact. I realised I was falling for her as wildly and uncontrollably as I had done for Kylie some three years before down under. I thought hearing my earlier warning to myself, at least she seems to like me enough. One other thing I had spotted on a more positive note, any thought of Kylie was not now filled with pangs of anguish. I was learning more about this man called Shane, when he falls, he falls hard, but it is curable! I looked at the small dark girl in front of me with the flashing eyes she was firing right back at me. "You're gorgeous," I shouted at her over the racket.

"I know, sickening isn't it," she shouted back with a dazzling smile that would be worth a million bucks a week in Hollywood. She mouthed something else, which might have been funny, if I could hear anything over the din coming out of the speakers.

With the next song the DJ played straight into my hands; it was a slow sweet number drenched in Hammond organ. She snuggled up close to me hanging round my neck with her slender arms. She looked up into my eyes, and kissed me. The various aromas from her, and her hair especially, were an intoxicating mixture. Behind the, not overpowering, smell she had acquired from a bottle, there was a much more fascinating scent which was obviously natural. By now I should have realised I was in desperate need of help. If her natural musk was having this effect on me, I was a lost cause. Still, the signals I was receiving from those brilliant eyes, and the light filigree kisses were all positive. "You're sweet," she said as she nuzzled my left ear, just as the music ended.

Maybe I could play vain too, "You know, you're the thirteenth girl who's said that to me today."

"That's unlucky. You poor boy having to get your kicks from counting how many girls say you're sweet. Haven't you got anything better to do?" She cocked her head on one side, and still ravaged me with her smile, but I was aware that I had not achieved any points with that one. I smiled weakly back and kissed her, but I was aware how much power I was under.

"Drink?" she said to me, and I nodded. We made our way out of the dance floor into a quieter room with a makeshift bar at the far end. We could at least hear ourselves think here. She asked for a brandy, which I thought was quite a strange choice to have when you were thirsty. Me, I had a pint of the local 'gnats', because, however odd it tasted, it was a cool watery liquid.

One had to be deaf dumb or blind to be unaware of the undercurrent. It had been obvious to me that it wasn't just her feelings for me that had led her to moving out of college where she had lived with her erstwhile friend, Liz, whom I had met on that first night what seemed like a lifetime ago. Jenny came from Norwich, and was Anglian through and through, and Liz was a Londoner and very English.

I looked across the bed at the sleeping form, which glowed at me in its nakedness. She didn't sweat, exactly; she just shone as if there was a light source deep inside her. She opened one eye; once again she had caught me looking at her. Guilty as charged, how could I not look at such beauty when it was there before my eyes? I wasn't just in love, I was addicted to this woman.

'Penny for your thoughts,' she whispered.

I thought for a moment and said, 'I was wondering what the odds were, that someone like you should be there and available when someone like me turned up. How come nobody had snaffled you up before I arrived?'

She gave me a look of infinite sadness for a moment, 'There was,' she said, 'but he died.' She paused for a moment, before throwing her arms round my neck and saying gently, 'and now I've got you,' and snuggled herself into me and kissed my ear.

When we woke again, you could tell there was something going on outside. There was a pod with a loudspeaker on its roof, explaining exactly how the locals should behave when the English Army arrived the following morning, and that from then on there would be a curfew from 6pm every evening, the breach of which would lead to immediate arrest.

That evening we spent in the pub down the road. Nobody felt much like live music, so the ambience was of the canned variety, while Ali joined us at our table. Jenny was quiet, almost disconcertingly so, while Ali and I discussed the plans we had for crack of dawn the following morning. He had already bought tickets for us to catch the milk train in the morning to Birmingham, where we would change for Shrewsbury, and points west. He passed me two tickets, one of which I slid into my pocket.

'I have to pick up one or two things before we go,' said Jenny popping the other ticket into her bag. 'If I don't see you both before, I'll see you at the train.' I could see she was tapping her wristy, summoning a pod.

The following morning was wet. The sky knew what was going to happen to its beloved Cambridge, and it couldn't control its tears. I looked at my wristy, and it was counting down to our departure time. I was standing by the Birmingham train, and people were rushing around me trying to get on board, while I jumped up and down to see over the top of them. It was at moments like this that I wished she was taller.

Ali pulled on my sleeve, 'Come on mate, it's time to go. If she was coming she would be here by now.'

My face was wet, whether it was the rain or my tears, I had no idea, she was coming, she had to be coming, we loved each other didn't we? She's been delayed, perhaps that's it. She'll be here any moment.

A man stood at the end of the platform and blew his whistle.

'Come on mate, time to go,' said Ali as he pulled me onto the train. As it pulled out of the station, I was still hanging out of the window, looking down the platform for the person who was nowhere to be seen.

§§§§

Flash forward to present day
I felt a tug at my shoulder, 'Shane ... Shane.'

I opened my eyes, and there she stood.

'Pull up a chair,' I said pushing the bottle and a glass towards her. 'Help yourself,' I slurred, 'I kept it for you.'

She ignored them. 'Shane,' she said, 'we need to talk.'

'What about?'

'Cambridge; I have a story to tell you.'

'Is it a good one, starting off with once a polly-tight-oh, like all good fairy stories should? Has it got any jokes in it? Right now I'm in need of a good joke.'

'Shane, stop it.' Her voice sounded cross. I looked at her face, and I knew she could take total control if I gave her an inch.

'Okay,' I said, 'tell me your story, and I'll tell you if I like it.'

'It's the story of a girl who met a rather wonderful older man, whom she first met at a meeting in Norwich. He was telling the audience about Anglia's newly won independence, and he fascinated her with his thoughts and philosophy on life. She was very young at that time, maybe ten or eleven, but she became infatuated with that man and over time, following him round to other places she thought she was in love with him. He helped the people of Wales and Wessex achieve their freedom too. Many people became, how do you put it, disenfranchised when the two main English political parties disintegrated and the ruins re-coalesced together to form a single party of government, to drive through Brexit and all the little bits of legislation that would be required to be discussed and passed in the minimal amount of time they had before B-day. That at least was how it should have been if there had been an opposition. But as there wasn't such a thing, those laws just passed themselves tick, tick, tick, and Bob's your uncle. They had a snap election immediately afterwards, far too quickly for any other new party of opposition to get itself together, and the land still voted Conservative or Labour, mostly blissfully unaware they were voting for the same thing, and that was the last election they ever had in England.

'Andrew helped set up pressure groups in local areas, and became something of a name. I suppose the first time I knew he had been arrested was in Maidstone when he was talking to a Home Counties group. He escaped from there and the next time they caught him was in Leeds, also preaching at a meeting, this time they accused him of inflaming the people of the Ridings of Yorkshire. I last heard of him being caught in Cheltenham in Arden, and I heard he was shot resisting arrest.'

'Good story, perhaps if one was to be picky, it could have done with a few more jokes here and there. Tell me what you think of my story, which also starts, "it's the story about a girl, who met a man," who thought she was rather wonderful, and then one day she simply wasn't there anymore and he was left on a train station dripping wet with a stupid expression on his face, because his guts had been ripped out. Not many laughs in my story, either I suppose.' I refilled my glass from the now nearly empty bottle.

'You don't understand. I became his muse, his icon of disenfranchised youth. I married him when we were in Scotland.'

'So you married him when you were in Scotland, and he got potted while he was running around upsetting the English. How many times did you tell that tale between his getting potted and your meeting me in Cambridge?'

She looked at me sadly. 'I could have told my story to the Shane I knew in Cambridge, and he would have understood. I haven't got a chance with the drunken photocopy sitting in front of me now, so I don't think I'll bother. Tell you something Shane; if I had known you were going to be in Holyhead, I would have done my level best not to come here. But actually, now that I have, I'm sort of relieved that I did. Just think what would have happened to me if you'd turned into this nasty vicious drunk sitting in front of me, while we were still together.' She stood up and walked away saying, 'Goodbye Shane, it was wonderful while it lasted.' And, without looking over her shoulder, even once, she eased out of the bar and into the night.

I watched her go. I picked up the two envelopes off the table, and while sliding them into my jacket breast pocket, I realised there was already an envelope in there. I pulled it out. It was those travel documents. They needed hiding properly, as Evans would be hunting for them high and low once he realised that McGregor no longer had them.

I was looking at the piano, and the piano looked back at me. I flipped up the top of the piano and slid the envelope in behind the strings. Nobody would think there was anything there, even if Ali was playing a Beethoven Sonata. Did Ali play any Beethoven? I had no idea. They might be difficult even for me to get them out again, and I knew they were there, but they were safe, and they might come in useful for Ali and me in the fullness of time.

I closed the top of the piano, and picked up the other two envelopes, and made my slightly unsteady way up the stairs to my flat to put them in a safe, and me into bed. I had enough whisky on board to guarantee that I fell asleep again.

§§§§

The following day was bright. Surprisingly I felt quite bouncy, considering how much I had put away the previous evening.

'Morning Shane,' said Geraint, our storekeeper from behind the bar.

'Morning G,' I replied.

'I was wondering whether our supply of Scotch has arrived at the Green Shamrock yet,' he said. 'Our stock level's running down.' He glanced at the nearly empty bottle of Ardbeg and the glasses, which had somehow made their way from the table by the piano back onto the bar. He didn't make any comment, but his thoughts were obvious enough.

'I'm in the mood for a walk this morning,' I said. 'I'll wander over. Oh and if the police want to look over the place, give them every assistance you can.'

He smiled at me, 'I always do,' he replied, 'but they never find anything. Anything in particular that you want them not to find today?'

I shrugged, 'Not that I can think of, but they arrested McGregor here last night so I expect they'll be looking for something.'

'Joey McGregor?' he asked and I nodded, 'Poor bastard,' he said after which there was little more that needed saying.

§§§§

The Green Shamrock isn't very far from the docks either. It is owned and run by a huge Irishman, called "Tubba" O'Laorie. I've no idea what his real name is, but he's known as "Tubba" to one and all in Holyhead, and believe me it's a respectful nickname. Nobody disrespects "Tubba" and gets away with it.

'Shane, you old bastard,' he shouted across the bar at me as I walked in.

'Tubba, you apology for a Leprechaun,' I replied, 'how you doing?'

'Come and sit with me,' he waved a huge paw at an empty table. 'Drink?'

'At this time in the morning, it's too early for anything other than coffee.'

He flicked his fingers at his barman, and called out, 'Coffee for one.' The barman stopped whatever it was he was doing, and went over to his barista machine. Any friend of Tubba's, you know the rest. The speed it took for the cup of coffee to arrive at my table was simply breath taking. If there had been a camera trained on that barman, he'd have got a ticket.

'So what can I do for you today?'

'I wondered if my supply of whisky had arrived yet?'

'You're in luck; it arrived yesterday. Straight off the boat from the islands.'

'Good, I'm told by my stock controller that my levels need replenishing. And, by the way, when I pay you for a dozen bottles, I really do expect to get a real dozen, and not a Tubba's dozen which is usually eleven, but it's not unknown to be even fewer.'

He shrugged, 'you know, we do have expenses to cover, people need bribing to turn blind eyes. You do know the Ardbeg you buy from me is real Ardbeg, not that knock off Islay Mist stuff, relabelled.' We both glared at each other for a moment, and then his voice became almost chirpy, 'I hear you had a little excitement last night at your place,' he said, 'an arrest or something.'

'Ah yes, poor old Joey,' I sighed. I tried to sound sad, but I'm really not that good an actor.

'And they said he was responsible for that courier

being knocked off his bike and killed for some travel documents he was carrying.'

'Is that was what it was about,' I said lazily, 'I did wonder.'

He grinned at me. 'I don't think for a moment you don't know exactly what's going on in your bar. I imagine you're also aware of who he had intended to get those documents to?'

'Oh?'

'There's a fellow in town called Andrew Ryan who I understand is desperate to get to Ireland PDQ, and I understand that Joey had got those documents for him.'

'Really? If they turn up I'll let you know.'

'If he turns up in your bar, you'll be a very rich man,' he said. 'Stop me if you've heard this before, but I don't suppose you'd like to come into partnership with me, would you?'

'And why would I want to do a thing like that? I'm scared enough of where I might end up every time I walk into your bar. They say that the last person who disagreed with you was found underneath the Menai Bridge wearing concrete wellies. At least they think it was him, the body was unrecognisable, but he was still identified by the expensive gold wristy he was wearing. Now I'm no detective, but I can't help thinking that a wristy like that would have been the first thing that anybody would steal if it was the straight robbery and murder they claimed it was. We both know you're a gangster Tubba.'

'True, true,' he nodded sagely, 'but isn't it better to be on the side of the devils and feel safe, than on the side of the angels and feel threatened?'

'I'm not on anybody's side,' I replied.

I finished my coffee, wiped my mouth, and grinned at him. 'That should do,' I remarked, standing up.

'What for?'

'I think Evans has much the same feeling that you do, that McGregor's mythical documents have somehow ended up in my bar. I needed to give them time to search the place. See you later with the whisky,' I said, and stood up. As I reached the door, who should I meet coming the other way, but Ryan and Jenny?

'The guy you're looking for is the fat drongo sitting over there,' I said to Ryan, and tossed a thumb at Tubba as I made my way out. I ignored Jenny completely.

§§§§

The first person I came face to face with when I got back was, you'll never guess, Rhys Evans. I was pleasantly surprised to see the police helping my staff reassemble the bar, and getting all the tables back in some sort of order. They had been thorough.

'Hello Shane, I saw you weren't here, been anywhere interesting?'

'You know I can't standing watching you and your goons go through my bar like a spinner through a batting side on a drying pitch. I went over to the Green Shamrock to have a coffee with my mate Tubba.'

'And, no doubt to check on the status of your illegal orders?' I raised an eyebrow. This was another of those things that we both knew, but as long as we didn't admit it, it didn't actually exist. I think the

44

phrase was plausible deniability. 'Time for another cuppa?' he added.

'Why not? Somehow I always prefer the stuff we serve here than the stuff he serves at the Shamrock. I think it's how we grind the beans. We crush the beans whereas he cuts through them with what is in effect an electric scythe. Our cell walls are still intact, but his are blasted to smithereens, which makes his coffee far more bitter.'

'I did wonder. I always assumed you get the beans from the same place; and yet somehow the result is quite different.'

'I have a deal with a man in Dublin; I think he gets the beans from Germany. Where they come from before then, I have no idea. It doesn't pay to ask, and if I buy enough for the Shamrock as well, it's cheaper that way for both of us.'

'It all got rather exciting here last night, didn't it, one way or the other, don't you think?'

'It had its moments. Just as a matter of interest, what's going to happen to McGregor?'

'Oh poor Joey. I'm afraid he didn't make it, poor lamb.'

'What does it say on his death certificate?'

'I haven't decided yet. It may say suicide, or it may say shot while resisting arrest. It might even say diabetic ketoacidosis.'

'I didn't know he was diabetic.'

'They say these things can come on awfully quickly. Anyway I suspect the Colonel will probably have the final say on that one.'

'As you say, very sad.'

'One thing, a propos of nothing in particular,' the policeman's tone changed quite sharply, 'they say he was carrying some travel documents that were stolen from the courier who was murdered in Bangor.'

'Joey? Did that? I never knew he had it in him.'

'So you don't know anything about those documents? And the reason that I ask, is that shortly after we apprehended Mister McGregor, who should walk into your bar but the famously indestructible Andrew Ryan. What do you think he might have been looking for in here do you think?'

'A drink? This is a bar you know.'

'Now I just know you're being flippant. No, he would have been coming in here to find McGregor to get those documents from him. Those Royal travel documents are the only ones for leaving Holyhead which don't have to be signed and rubber stamped by me.'

'Really? Do tell.'

'When they shipped the Queen and the other Royals off to Canada after Brexit, ostensibly to keep them safe during the period of unrest...'

'Was there unrest? I was a kid in Adelaide, down under, at the time. So I wasn't interested in the newspapers apart from the sport and the funny pages.'

'The army was out and about, much as they are today, and there was a curfew, but not a lot else. Anyway, as things calmed down, the Royals were allowed back into the country. They're harmless enough, and they're good for business as far as the English are concerned. They even have royal castles in Anglia and Scotland, and every bit of Royalty brings money into the island from outside. The Western folks like us, the Irish and the Wessexmen, don't have a lot to do with them, but we do allow them to travel in and out of our countries without rocking any apple carts, and they have their own official travel documents.'

'Fascinating, so that's what it was all about. And our favourite Mister Ryan is pretending to get to Ireland on a Royal pass?'

'Got it in one.'

'Does he look like a Royal? You know receding chin, jug ears and the rest? And Jenny, which Royal would she pass for, for Gods sake?'

'Ah well, they don't have pictures on or anything like that, merely a statement that it requires all whom it may concern to allow the bearer to pass freely without let or hindrance, and to afford their bearer such assistance and protection as may be necessary.'

'Ah.'

'The bottom line is this. I would really rather that Ryan never gets to Ireland.'

'He's a slippery bastard isn't he? I've lost count of the number of times he's been reported dead, and then up he bobs still alive somewhere else.'

'Oh, I'm not planning on killing him. I want him to become a permanent resident here in Holyhead. How would you like that? Ryan and that lovely girl a permanent fixture in your bar? I thought you'd enjoy that. You run a casino, they tell me. How would you fancy a little wager?'

'I run a casino, so I know exactly how they work. You don't think I'd be stupid enough to gamble in one do you?'

'You'll like this one. I'll bet you that Ryan will get out of Holyhead into Ireland.'

'Huh?'

'I bet you that he will, so if he fails to get to

47

Ireland, you win.'

'How much are we talking here Rhys?'

'Ten thousand a year?'

'Wow! You are serious; make it twenty and you're on.'

'You drive a hard bargain. You do know I'm only a poor corrupt policeman don't you?'

'Most of that, apart from the "poor" bit.'

'We have a deal?'

'We have a deal.' And with that, we shook hands, and he followed his policemen out of my bar.

§§§§

I took the empty cups over to the bar, and I was just about to go upstairs, and how do you say it, powder my nose, when I heard, 'Are you Mister Shane?'

She was small, blonde and pretty in a way that was far too young to be in a bar. 'How did you get in here?' I asked, 'There is a minimum age limit to be allowed into bars in Wales you know.'

'I came in to find Inspector Evans,' she replied. 'I was told to meet him here.'

Oh, that's how it was, was it? 'Go on.' I said encouraging her to continue.

'How trustworthy do you think the Inspector is?' she asked.

'I think if he has promised to do something, you can pretty much count on his doing it.'

She thought for a moment, and then continued. 'I thought that might be the case.' She paused and then looked at me directly with eyes that were far too big for her best interests. 'You're a man of the world Mr Shane, aren't you?' This was getting awkward, and I sort of half guessed where this was heading.

'Go on,' I said.

'If you did something really bad but for all the right reasons, and nobody knew, then that would be all right wouldn't it?'

'And you're trying to get to Ireland…'

'…to catch the Airship to America yes. And it's so difficult to get two tickets.'

'Two?' I asked, looking at her, there was scarcely enough in that package to merit one ticket, let alone two.

'I'm going with my boyfriend. He has relations in Cleveland Ohio. I'm told it's safe there. But in some ways, he's terribly young, and very possessive, but he's so sweet. And he'd never know. I mean, who would tell him? There's nobody we'll meet here we'll ever meet in Cleveland, and over there, who's ever heard of Holyhead?'

'And you want my permission?'

'No, yes, oh I don't know.' She looked on the verge of tears.

'Have you any idea what it is you're being asked to do?'

'Yes, no. But I'm told it's very nice, you know, the best thing that two people can do together.'

Oh for crying out loud! 'Where have you two come from?'

'Ilford, in Essex.'

'And you want my advice?'

'Yes.'

'Go back to Ilford.'

'But I can't. Joshy's in your casino trying to win the money to pay Inspector Evans for the passes, but you and I know how casinos work, don't we? He hasn't got a snowball's chance in hell of winning that sort of money has he?'

'He's in my casino, you say?'

'Yes,'

'Follow me.'

It was impossible not to tell who 'Joshy' was. He was by some ten years the youngest person in the room. He still had some acne, and was still several years short of growing a half acceptable moustache, although he was trying. He was sitting by the roulette table, looking seriously anxious. You really should never gamble with money you can't afford to lose.

I walked up behind him, catching Raoul's eye. 'Have you tried Number 10 yet? I have a gut feeling that it's going to come up shortly.' I said into his ear.

'But I…' he stammered.

'Number 10.' I said sharply, and he pushed his chips onto number 10.

'*Les jeux sont faits. Rien ne va plus*,' said Raoul instantly, telling the one or two other players dithering round the table that no further bets would be accepted for that spin of the wheel. He then gave it a good spin with his right hand, while his left hand went out of sight beneath the table's rim. When the wheel stopped, there was the little white ball, nestling in number 10. '*Numéro Dix*,' he said, '*noir et pair.*'

The boy was about to grab the chips off the table, still not understanding his 'luck.' 'Leave them,' I snapped, and Raoul had already started spinning the wheel. The boy looked at me, and looked at Raoul, and obviously still hadn't the faintest idea what was going on.

'*Numéro Dix,* said Raoul again, '*noir et pair.*'

'Now,' I said to the boy, 'take those chips to the

cashier and cash them out. Don't come back. Hopefully you will have a wonderful rest of your life in America.' He grabbed at his chips and rushed up to the till.

The tiny blonde sidled up to me, 'Thank you Mr Shane, thank you, I don't know how to thank you.'

'Don't mention it,' I thought for a moment and then added, 'ever.'

She rushed over to where Evans was sitting looking at the menu and contemplating what he was going to have for lunch. 'Inspector Evans,' she bounced at him, 'I've got your money. I'll be round by your office, promptly at eight o'clock tomorrow morning.'

'And I shall be there at ten,' he replied acidly, getting up and wandering over to where I was standing. 'You know you can be irritatingly ethical when you really put your mind to it,' he said. 'I've got a spectacularly athletic redhead coming in tomorrow, and if you interfere with her too, I might persuade myself not to overlook some of the discrepancies I have a habit of overlooking, if you see what I mean?'

Oh yes, I saw what he meant, Grown-ups can look after themselves, but really; those kids really were little more than children.

Raoul tapped on my shoulder, 'Shane, can I have a word?'

I looked at Raoul, 'How are we doing mate?' I asked grimly.

'Not as well as I would have predicted at the beginning of this week,' was his dry reply. 'Have you still got that envelope I gave you last night?'

'Sure, I haven't banked it yet.'

'Good, even a trivial win by Inspector Evans

would embarrass our float right now.'

'Say no more, I'll go and fetch it right away,' and I did just that. I went up to my office, opened the safe and got the envelope marked 'casino' out of it. I scribbled on the envelope, 'Takings zero', opened the envelope and put the cash in my pocket. The envelope went back into my safe to remind me what had happened and when, as a memento for my next meeting with the taxman.

I walked back down the stairs again and the place was beginning to fill up with lunchtime customers. Evans was already wrapping himself round the choicest cut of the day. We couldn't keep our promise to give him the best meal in the house if somebody had already eaten it, so he did meet us half way and come in early. I wandered back into the casino, and passed the contents of my pocket to Raoul, and he went straight into the place we jokingly called 'The Chip Shop,' and stowed it safely.

Another reason for the bar feeling full was that Tubba was there, complete with an even more massive sidekick, only this sidekick wasn't constructed from lipids, but from several tons of mineral and protein. He was carrying a crate of whisky on each shoulder. 'Ere, Guv, where d'you wann'um?' the stevedore asked Geraint behind the bar, suggesting that most of his electrical tissue was used for power rather than problem solving, and they both disappeared down, out of sight into the cellar.

'Shane, look, I'm as good as my word. Four cases of the finest Ardbeg.'

'And you wonder why everyone's terrified of you Tubba? The size of that man, it's more terrifying than Mitchell Starc steaming in at you at full chat.'

'I take it that that's one of your cricket metaphors,' he replied. I don't really get them you know.'

'But you play cricket in Ireland. Right now you've got a damn good team, far better than that shower the Poms fielded the other day. Absolutely wrecked by the Yanks they were.'

'I did always say that when the United States did finally start playing cricket properly instead of claiming that their Baseball tournament was a World Series, they'd probably get quite good at it. Oh very good! I see what you did there, very clever. Of course I follow cricket, who doesn't?' He looked around us, giving me a big fat hint that he was in the process of changing the subject. 'To be sure this is a nice place. Tell you something, I'll give you double what you paid for the place, right now cash in hand.'

'Not difficult Tubba, I never paid for it.'

'You mean old Aunty Eluned just gave you the place? I never knew. Why would she do a thing like that?'

'I don't think she liked you very much Tubba, and she did know Ali and I had some really good plans for it.'

'And so you did, and here they are for the whole world to see. If you won't sell me the place, how about me putting in a bid for Ali's services instead? He adds a touch of class to a place with all that ivory work. Do you think he'd come and work for me?'

'Why don't we ask him?'

We walked over to the piano where Ali was sitting doodling something to himself. 'Ali,' I said, 'Tubba is asking whether you'd like to go and work at the Green Shamrock.'

'Must I Shane? I'd much rather work here.'

'He'll pay you three times as much as I do you know,' I grinned at the look of surprise on Tubba's jowls.

'I don't get to spend all the money I earn here anyway,' he said, 'and besides I'd still get to play on Aunt Shazia if I stayed here.' He caressed the piano.

'I'll buy you that piano,' said Tubba.

'Aunt Shazia's an old lady, man. She'd never survive being wheeled round to the Shamrock without falling to pieces.

Tubba and I shrugged at each other. 'Well you can't blame a man for trying,' he said. The Stevedore was coming up from the cellar again. 'Weww, vat's ve whisky sorted boss,' he said through the relatively few teeth he'd got left.

'Did the coffee arrive?' Tubba asked.

'It's in the kitchen,' I said. 'Follow me.'

'Go along, follow him,' Tubba said crossly to the man-mountain who hadn't moved. We walked through the door, and I subconsciously checked that the frame was still in one piece after he had passed through it. It was, but it was a close thing. I pointed to three large hessian bags on the counter. He picked them all up at once, to the amazement of the chef, and walked out again.

'Handy to have one of those,' remarked the chef.

'Can't think when I'd ever use one,' I replied, 'apart from once a month at delivery time, and I always know where I can borrow it if it's needed.'

'Once again it's been a pleasure doing business with you,' said Tubba, tapping his wristy, and showing me the numbers on its face. 'That's what it looks like altogether.' I checked, and was tempted to knock off a nought, just to see what he would do. But then I could see the stevedore was watching us, and thought better of it. Those numbers were acceptable, and so I accessed my wristy and transferred the money across.

Tubba followed his man, loaded with bags of coffee, but not laden with them, if you see what I mean, out of the front door. He passed a man coming in, 'That's him over there,' he said pointing at me, 'by the piano.'

He had met Ryan at the door.

I pointed at a choice of tables, but he said, 'I'm not here for lunch. Is there anywhere we can go and talk, which isn't so overlooked?'

'My office, if you like. Follow me,' and we walked up the stairs and into my holy of holies. It really was private. It had a camera that looked straight down the stairs, and there was a monitor over the door. There was also a sensor under the third step which made a fairly polite noise through the monitor to tell me that someone was on the way up. Up until now, I had always managed to get the other half of an illicit tryst into my bedroom before the main door opened. 'What can I do for you?'

'I'll get straight to the point, I came to your bar yesterday to meet a man called McGregor.'

'Ah yes, poor Joey, so sad.'

'Quite,' he said not swallowing my sympathy for a moment. 'And this fellow McGregor had a couple of Royal Transport documents for me.'

'Uhuh.'

'They weren't on him when, um whatever happened to him happened to him.'

'When they killed him, you mean?'

'I wasn't sure you knew.'

'I think that you can safely count on the fact that I

know about most things that happen here in Holyhead.'

'So I'm led to understand. So, to cut a long story short; you've got those documents and I want them. How much?'

'You think I've got the documents? Joey McGregor came in here yesterday, and got arrested. They killed him, but didn't find those documents on him, and now everybody assumes that I've got them. Why is that?'

'Haven't you? How does half a million sound to you?'

Whoa! Talk about starting low and working up until a mid point is met that's acceptable to both parties. How far was this joker going to get to? He had that sort of backing behind him? He was now considerably scarier than Tubba with all his hired muscle.

I looked at him quizzically and didn't say anything, partly because an image of Jenny was flitting before my eyes, and somehow I couldn't help wanting to see her again, and again. 'You do know who I am?' he asked rather petulantly like an over-educated toff who felt whatever he wanted was his by right.

'Yes,' I said, 'I know who you are. Do you know who I am?'

'You're the Australian, who, right now, holds the fate of the free world in his hands.' This drongo really did have a high opinion of himself didn't he? Probably higher than anyone else, bearing in mind that to most people, myself included, he was some sort of hero. Mind you, given the fact that he had pulled Genevieve Laing before I had, maybe he did have some right to that opinion. However my opinion of him as a person was dropping fast.

'With the best will in the world,' I said slowly, 'and if, of course, just as a matter of argument, let's say I do have those documents, or at least know where they are; why would I not be saving them for my own personal use? In the fullness of time I might need to get out of North Wales in a hurry? From your own perspective, you can tell it's not an inconceivable question.'

He looked me straight in the eye, and replied, 'a million.'

'My final answer remains no.' I snapped, aware I was losing my temper.

'For God's sake, you could buy one of the Welsh Police's documents for a hundredth of that price.'

'So could you.'

'No I can't. It was made abundantly clear to me by both the Inspector and the British Colonel this morning, that I have absolutely no chance of getting one of those Welsh travel documents. So why won't you sell me yours?'

My stack just blew, 'May I suggest you ask your wife,' I said.

'My wife?' He looked puzzled.

'Your wife,' I replied and explained to him how the door to my flat worked.

§§§§

The bar had well filled up by the time I followed him out of the front door to my flat. He had got perhaps two steps down my stairs when a large man in an English Army uniform started singing 'Land of Hope and Glory' at his table. Ryan had barely descended two more steps when the whole table caught in on the act. I had rather hoped they might pull him into some semblance of tune, but hope like that rarely happens. It was just a louder bunch of crows cawing.

My brain was sensitive to the atmosphere in my bar, and I could already feel an uncertainty about it, maybe a sort of instability. I tried to catch Ali's eye to hint that he might play that thumping syncopated version of 'Waltzing Matilda' that he had once come up with to amuse me. We had found that ever since we took over the place it was an excellent peacemaker, as it was generally considered that Ali was taking the mick out of me, and somehow the Welsh thought that was funny.

I was also aware that Ryan was accelerating towards Ali, and that Ali was aware he was coming. Ryan bent down and said something to him, and then walked over to a group of Welsh Policeman standing near the bar. He raised his hand and started singing;

Wele'n, sefyll rhwng y myrtwydd
Wrthrych teilwng o fy myrd,
Er o'r braidd 'rwy'n Ei adnabod
Ef uwchlaw gwrthychau'r byd:
Henffych fore! Hennfych fore!
Caf ei weled fel y mae.
Caf ei weled fel y mae.' [1]

By the time the verse was finished, the whole room was ablaze with the sound of a Welsh Male Voice Choir at full throttle, with the full four parts and more heard on the *'caf ei weled'* bits. I could even see young Myfanwy singing at the top of her voice behind the bar. I had no idea what any of them were singing about, but it was stirring stuff, and I was really impressed, at least I was until a shot rang out, and the bar was bathed in instant silence.

Not far from the table where the English soldiers who started the sing song stood Colonel Willoughby. He was purple with rage, and he held a pistol from whose barrel a curl of smoke was visible.

I was down the rest of my stairs in a flash. I didn't care who he was, or which government he claimed to represent. Nobody was going to fire guns in my bar and get away with it; certainly not for the second day on the bounce.

Rhys Evans beat me to him.

'Don't worry,' said the Colonel. 'I only fired a blank.' That was probably aimed at me, as I was half looking for holes in my ceiling. 'I wanted to get your attention.'

'You've got it boyo,' said Evans. 'I have to say, I really rather enjoyed the singing. I didn't know we had so many people here in Holyhead who know the words to the Cwm Rhondda.'

'It would be an interesting test to see if they know the words of the second or subsequent verses,' I remarked cheerfully. 'Same with the Poms, they all know the words to the first verse of God Save the King, but the rest of them, not a chance, not even the 'knavish tricks' bit.'

I had no idea I was making things worse, but Evans obviously did, as he said sharply, 'When you're already in a hole, you idiot, stop digging!'

'I think we must reconsider our plans about Ryan,' said the still purple Willoughby. 'I don't think we can afford to keep him here in Holyhead indefinitely. If he can wind up your police in a single day, just think what he might achieve if he's still here in a month.'

'But..' Evans started to say.

'And I want this bar shut now. It's a hive of

dissidence and revolutionary fever.'

'Now look here,' I began.

Evans looked at me, and then the Colonel, and then his face changed. 'What!' he said very loudly, 'It appears that gambling is going on in this place. That's against the law! I declare this bar closed forthwith.'

'Your winnings, Inspector Evans,' said Raoul, sidling up to the policeman and putting a bulging fist into his pocket. It was less bulging when it was removed.

'Thank you Raoul,' said the Inspector. 'Now clear the bar. Everybody out.' He looked at the English Soldiers, 'You too. This place is now closed by order of the Welsh Police by order of...' blah blah bliddy blah. Evans had the bollocracy off pat.

§§§§

[1] Lo between the myrtles standing,
One who merits well my love,
Though His worth I guess but dimly,
High all Earthly things above.
Happy Morning! Happy Morning!
When at last I see him clear!
When at last I see him clear!

William Williams Pantycelyn (1762) Translated Peter Williams (1722-96)

§§§§

And suddenly the place was empty apart from me and my rather stunned looking staff.

I said to the assembled company. 'Sorry about that.'

'I don't see how any of that was your fault,' said

Raoul, all trace of any French accent now missing from his speech.

'How much food have you got ready?' I looked at the chef, 'that won't go back into storage?' I asked.

'About a dozen plates,' said his wife. 'We can put the rest back in the fridge for later. It'll need eating soon though.'

'I hope you can all face a spot of lunch over the next few days,' I said to everybody. 'It's on the house.'

There was a hubbub of 'thank you very muches' and the like; they sounded like a chorus of Elvises. I turned to Paul. 'How's it looking financially?'

'We're okay at the moment,' he said and grinned, 'despite some strange occurrences in the Casino over the past twenty-four hours.

'Good,' I replied. 'In which case, you're all still on salary, unless you want to go somewhere else, until I can work out exactly who needs bribing, and how much.'

'Surely it's Rhys Evans you've got to bribe,' Ali started.

'It's not quite so simple. He put on the show just now, true, but he was told to shut us down by that English Colonel chope. It's becoming clearer by the day who really rules the roost here on Holy Island, and I'm fairly sure they're not based in Caerdydd.'

The lunch settled down to being a group of friends quietly licking their wounds together, and talking about anything but the elephant in the room, as friends do. Once the eating had been done and the bar had been tidied, everybody quietly and sheepishly left the building, leaving just me and old Paul kicking the can down the road and drinking one final cup of coffee, before he too set off to wherever he was planning to go. I insisted that I shouldn't know where that might be in case my discussion with Rhys Evans or with whoever it was I would need to transfer funds to, didn't go quite according to plan. Plausible deniability, and any other clichés you can pull off the top of your head.

He was leaving by the main door, when I heard him say, 'he's over by the piano.'

I didn't need to look at the person coming in to know who it was. It was a little earlier than I had anticipated, true, but I had known this conversation was going to take place as soon as I saw her yesterday. And I knew it was her simply because of the aura of magic she always carried with her. She didn't need a scent, as an early warning siren. She just had 'it'. I can't remember when I first became aware of it, maybe the second time we met, maybe the third, but once I had been bitten, there was never going to be anyone else, ever.

'Hello Shane,' she said in a soft voice like silk as she walked over to where I was sitting. I hadn't stood up. I know that was impolite of me, but I was still trying to maintain some sort of control.

'Hello, my precious,' I said trying to sound like Smeagol. 'Do you want a coffee or anything stronger?' I offered.

'I don't think so, I just wanted to see you.'

'And here I am. What do you want to see me about?'

'I want those travel documents, Shane.'

I laughed drily. 'The travel documents, the travel documents. It's always the bloody travel documents. It seems that as long as people think I have those travel documents, I'll never be on my own.'

'You know that's not fair Shane. I only want one for Andrew, and I'll give you anything for that. Just tell me what you want. Anything,' she repeated slowly.

'I don't know that I want anything right now. I've got everything I need. Look.' And I waved an expansive paw all around the bar. 'All mine.'

'I don't see any customers Shane.'

'That's a rather a cheap shot, but it's only a temporary glitch, nothing to worry your head about.'

'You're going to have to come up with a big bribe to reopen your pub, and that might be a little difficult while Andrew is still around. You know we can sort that out between us now.'

'What, you give me loads of money, I give you the tickets, you both disappear, and my pub gets reopened, simple as that!'

'Just one ticket will be enough.'

'You mean, you're going to take a powder, and you're leaving poor old Ryan here to face the music. That's a side to you I wasn't previously aware of. You really are some kind of mercenary Mata Hari, aren't you? I supposed it was always going to be this way. In every relationship there's always someone who does the loving, and there's the other one who just lets it happen.'

It sounded like a sob that turned into a snarl. 'Just give me those fucking tickets,' she spat at me. And then I realised she was holding a revolver, and it was pointed straight at me.

'Dingo's kidneys.' I said, 'You've learned some new cuss words since we were together.' I walked slowly towards her. 'Now bring your hand up a little,' I said. Her hand shook slightly, as I lifted the business end of the revolver a touch. 'There,' I said, 'that's it.

Now all you need to do is squeeze the trigger, gently, and you'll be putting me out of my misery.'

She was still shaking and said, 'Go and get those documents.'

I put my hand over my jacket pocket. 'I don't have to go anywhere, they're right here. I suppose you'd have to miss them when you shoot me, I don't know how valid they would be covered in blood, with a bullet hole through them. Some Customs officers might think there was something, shall we say, not quite bonzer about them in that condition.'

'Stop it Shane....' she blurted.

'Just pull the bloody trigger, woman!' We were so close at that point that one of only two things could possibly have happened, and the fact that I'm here telling you all this will tell you what actually did. She dropped the gun, and threw herself into my arms and kissed me.

You think I could resist that? This was the one woman I loved most in my entire life, and she was kissing me? She pulled away for a moment and gave me both barrels with those fabulous eyes, and then rushed back in. After a moment, she said. 'I think we should go up to your flat. Someone might come in, and I don't think either of us would be able to stop.'

I followed her up the stairs and opened my flat. It took me a moment, but when we got up there, I sank down in the chair behind my desk and pulling the envelope out of my pocket, I slapped it on my desk. 'I've got to hand it to you kid,' I said acidly, 'you're good.'

'What? You think that was a payment for those tickets do you?'

'Wasn't it?'

She smiled at me softly. 'You silly old pillock. Of course it wasn't. Don't you realise that it's you I'm in love with; it's only ever been you, right since that first day at the meat market? Come here.'

A spot more kissing took place, and then I pulled back. 'So what about Ryan?' I asked, 'I still don't understand.'

'As I said, I was very young when I met him. It was terribly exciting being involved with a dangerous, revolutionary figure. Do you remember all those posters students at university had on their walls, the one of Che Guevara? I was a kid who had got herself a real live Che Guevara. And then he got caught, and I heard he had died resisting arrest, and much to my relief, I grew up and went to university. On my first day there, I met you. And the rest is history.'

'So everything we had in Cambridge was genuine?'

'Yes,' she looked worried for a moment, 'Wasn't it for you too?'

I smiled, 'and then some,' I replied. 'I couldn't think of anything else. So what happened?'

'You know that day when you, Ali and I were planning to come west the following morning, I met Liz in the street for the first time in a long time. She told me that Andrew had escaped, but only just, and was hiding somewhere near Lincoln gravely ill, and he needed me. She made it sound like he was on the way out, and he wanted to say, you know, goodbye. I left that afternoon. I think it had still been my intention to join you and Ali at the station the following morning.'

'So, what happened?'

'As you can see, the one thing he never actually did was die. I ended up nursing him back to health.

65

Travelling secretly through Lincolnshire, I realised how desperate the rest of the country was. We were comfortable and warm in Norwich and Cambridge. It wasn't until I saw the real England that I realised how poor and downright dangerous the place was. There were scruffy kids starving, and begging in the streets. There weren't any police, just the Army wandering about in squads, amusing themselves by abusing the locals. The only vehicles about weren't those dinky little electric pods we had in Anglia, and we have here in Wales, they were big smelly armoured cars that belch black fumes, and usually with a massive gun mounted on the front of a turret. Those people needed a hero, someone to believe in, someone to rescue them, and that person was lying, feverish in the bed in front of me. Do you think I could abandon him then?'

I saw her point. Certainly the Jenny I thought I knew couldn't do that. I looked at her and adored her even more at that moment than I ever really thought I had done before. Was that possible?

'But he's well now,' she continued, 'and he doesn't need me anymore, and you and I found each other again. Oh Shane, just hold me, as if it's the last opportunity we'll ever have.' And she started unbuttoning my shirt.

§§§§

I looked at her, just as I had done before. Her body was still the most beautiful thing I had ever seen, and it still shone like it had some strange internal light source. I am probably exaggerating a bit here; it was probably the moonlight coming through the open window that was reflecting off her perfect skin.

While I was just gently gaping, I became aware of some activity on the monitor in the next room. I slipped out of bed without disturbing her, and walked into my office, pulling on the dressing gown I had hanging on the back of the bedroom door.

I sat down at my desk and watched the screen carefully. The old chap pouring the drinks was Paul, anyone could see that, but who as the other guy? At one moment he glanced up at the camera. He probably wasn't even aware it was there, but at that point I knew exactly who it was. I went back into the bedroom and touched Jenny softly on her wonderful shoulder.

'Mmm?' She mumbled.

'You've got to get up,' I said softly.

She took that as an invitation and threw a sleepy arm round my neck, 'Tiger man!' she grinned, 'you have no idea how much I love you right now.'

You have no idea how tempted I was at that moment just to throw caution to the winds. But I said, 'you've got to get up. Something's come up. Get dressed.' And she could see I was serious. I got dressed myself, intentionally not watching her. I still wasn't sure whether I could keep my hands off her if I saw her actually covering herself up.

'What?' she said after fully reassembling herself.

I led her to the office and pointed at the monitor. She saw immediately what I was looking at and said, 'Oh shit.'

'Quite,' I agreed suddenly thinking ridiculously quickly for someone who was asleep a few moments ago. 'Go back to the bedroom, I'll see if I can attract Paul's attention.'

She went back into the room and I threw open the office door. 'Paul,' I bellowed, 'Can I see you up here for a moment.'

They both made a move for the stairs. 'No just Paul, I'll be down to join you in a moment.'

Paul made his way up the stairs and into the office, shutting the door behind him. 'Yes Shane?' he said quizzically, suddenly becoming aware of the figure standing behind me. His mouth formed a perfect circle in surprise, but he didn't say anything.

'Paul, you know all the alleyways and byways of this town by heart don't you?'

'I would think so Shane, yes.'

'Can you get Miss Laing back to her hotel without getting either of you caught?'

'Piece of cake.'

'Right, I'll see you when you get back.'

Our parting kiss was rather a tame affair after what had gone on before, but what was probably more lingering was the 'See you tomorrows,' we both said. And through the back door, they were gone.

I opened the front door of my office and went down the stairs. Ryan was down by the bar trying to single handedly put a plaster on his left wrist.

'Here, let me help,' I said.

'Thank you very much.'

'That looked nasty.'

'I had to climb through a window. I think they were waiting for us.'

'The Police?'

'The Police, the Army, Uncle Tom Cobbleigh and all. Suddenly they were everywhere. Somebody had grassed us up.'

'Aren't there times like this when you really

wonder whether it's all worth it, doing this thing that you do?'

He looked at me and smiled, 'It's what I do. It's my reason for getting up every morning.' He looked at me silently for a moment and then added, 'Can I tell you a story?'

'Why not? Everybody else seems to want to tell me stories.'

'Not very long ago I was passing through a midland town, and I saw an aging Asian man, sitting outside a chip shop with his family. At least I assumed they were his family. They were sitting with him, their faces covered in the full niqab, so you couldn't see their faces. But the rest of them wasn't covered by very much. Some of those kids were paler than others. While I was passing, a man in uniform walked up and gave him some money. The soldier looked at the kids for a moment, and selected one, who immediately trotted off behind him. The Asian then gave the money to one of the other kids, who rushed into the chip shop to buy some chips. Can't you see what sort of country this place has become where a man is forced to sell the bodies of his children to get food for the others?'

'Nasty,' I said.

'And you ask why I bother? It's not as if you're entirely innocent of caring either, Shane,' he remarked drily.

'What do you mean by that?'

'I was watching your performance with that little blonde kid today. That wasn't the action of a man who doesn't give a damn about the state of the world.'

'We all have occasional lapses. She was a pretty

little thing, after all.'

'Oh right, and you want me to believe that's why you did it?' I shrugged. 'I know quite a lot of things about you, Shane,' he continued.

'You do?'

'I knew for a fact that you are in love with a woman, who means the world to you, and that interestingly enough, she's the same woman I'm in love with. I don't actually have a problem with that. In fact, every day I'm secretly surprised that there aren't more people out there who feel the same way about her that I do. Now I realise you're not going to let *me* have those travel documents, but seriously are you going to keep her here just because of me? Give her one of those documents and at least let her get off this godforsaken island.'

'You love her that much?'

'You may see me as just a warrior standing for a cause. Well I'm a human being too, and, yes, I love her that much.'

The conversation might have gone on forever, but that wasn't to be. The front doors flew open, and in walked three rather burly men wearing the uniform of the Welsh border police. 'Mister Ryan? You're under arrest,' said the one in front.

'On what charge?'

'Take your pick,' replied the NCO, 'Shall we say being an enemy of the people, for now?'

Ryan looked at me, and I shrugged. What else was there to say?

§§§§

'Shane, Listen. There's no point in going on about it,' Rhys Evans could look quite cross when he wanted to. 'Why are you getting so agitated anyway? We both

70

know you've got a thing about his woman? Surely everything would be better without him being around and in the way?'

'But that's just it. He will still be around. What evidence have you actually got? Probably enough to keep him behind bars for a week or so top whack, and then he'll be out again, glaring balefully at us across some bar or another. That won't be good enough for anybody, for you, me or anybody else for that matter.'

'You've piqued my interest, what have you got in mind?'

'Let him go now, and we'll see if we can't come up with something better, shall we say, a rather more permanent solution to our problem?'

'I think Colonel Willoughby would have an apoplectic fit if we released him right now.'

'Really? I thought he was going to have one yesterday to be honest, and I was quite looking forward to seeing what happened when his head exploded. Oh, come on Rhys, you can't say that that thought doesn't amuse you? Oh come on, don't tell me you like the chope?'

'Nothing could be further from the truth, I can't stand the man.'

'There you go then. Explain to the drongo, that you have a plan to stitch Ryan up permanently, but the only way you can do that is to let him back on the streets for the moment.'

'Go on.'

'You've probably guessed the least well kept secret in Holyhead at the moment.'

'What? You mean that you've got those travel documents? Yes, I must ask you about them sometime.'

'What you really need is for them to be found in Ryan's possession when you next arrest him. You might even make it stick that he was responsible for killing that unfortunate courier. Accessory to murder would probably cook his goose.'

'You know you really are a tricky customer, Shane. Tell me, you'd do all that for a woman?'

'Come on Rhys, you've seen her, and it's me she wants, not him. This will help everybody. Just let it fly, what have you got to lose? Now he's a tricky bloke, so you've got to be careful. We don't want him smelling a rat before we catch him.'

'So what have you got in mind?'

'Get someone not wearing a uniform to tell him to meet me at the docks at five o'clock this evening, just before the high tide sailing, and I'll have the documents ready for him when he gets there. Meanwhile, while we're round and about today, keep your goons off the street. It won't do the plan any good if I'm arrested with the documents in my possession before the handover, will it?'

'But if Ryan leaves Holyhead for any reason, you'll lose our bet. You do realise that don't you?'

'You've seen Jenny Laing. Don't you think that a lifetime with that wouldn't trump any stupid little bet that you and I might have? Oh and one other thing, perhaps you might also see your way clear to allowing my bar to reopen its doors, as a little extra thank you for helping you over this.'

'You're really quite a nasty piece of work, under that veneer of Australian cultivation, aren't you Shane.' He looked at me, and shrugged, 'Very well, let's get on with it.'

§§§§

72

My next port of call was the Green Shamrock. Tubba was there slurping a mug of coffee as I walked in. 'Is that offer still open?' I asked, offering him the use of my hand.

'I hope you're not expecting me to have that kind of cash on my person,' he replied, acknowledging both my question and me.

'To be honest, I'd be surprised if you didn't somewhere, but as long as your wristy is as trustworthy as mine, I can cope with it just being an electronic credit transfer.'

We held our wrists together in a moment that would have looked very camp in times other than our own. 'By the way, you do know that Ali gets twenty-five per cent of the net profits don't you?'

'I happen to know it's only ten per cent. But whatever you say is all right with me. You know something Shane; it's going to be an emptier place without having you around. I really hope she's worth it.'

I looked at him, possibly slightly wistfully for a moment, and then said, 'So do I Tubba, so do I.'

§§§§

It was one of those drizzling afternoons that the British Isles are so famous for as I walked back to the bar. It was strange walking in there and seeing nothing going on. I walked up the stairs to my office and sat down at the desk for a moment. I have to say I was feeling kind of wistful when I looked round for the last time. As I did, something caught my eye. It was Jenny's revolver, still on the side stand where she had put it down last night and after one thing or another we had both forgotten all about it. I picked it up, and flipped it open. I wasn't actually expecting it to be loaded, but it was, all six chambers, and as I flicked them out I realised they weren't blanks. It was a chilling experience just looking at them. She had been prepared to shoot me when she came round last night. You don't carry around a loaded gun unless you're prepared to use it; right? I thought about it for a moment, flipped it back together, and dropped it into my pocket. Well if she had come loaded for bear, then perhaps I ought to too. At the very least I could return it to her. She might have use for it further down the line.

The documents I slipped into the inside pocket of my jacket, and turning slowly on my heel, muttering a slightly sad farewell to the place, I made my way down the back staircase and wandered off towards the docks.

I ambled into the departure lounge, certainly aware that there didn't appear to be even a minimal police presence about. Rhys appeared to have been as good as his word, at least until I entered the rather scruffy departure lounge itself. When I walked in, there was Rhys Evans, sitting in a chair facing the door.

'Oh there you are Shane,' he said. 'For a moment I was beginning to think you had stood me up.'

I looked at him for a moment, and asked lazily, why he thought I might do something stupid like that?

'You've got the documents?' he asked. I looked at him for a moment and then looked around the room. Well, I suppose this was the moment of truth. If it was all about those travel documents, then I was stuffed. I had to just hope that it really was Ryan he was after. I tapped my left breast, and he looked up at me. 'All safe and sound?'

'All safe and sound,' I replied.

He smiled and then asked, 'satisfy my curiosity. When we searched the place, we couldn't find those documents anywhere; where did you hide them?'

'In Ali's piano,' I replied.

'Serves me right for not being musical,' he said with a chuckle. He looked up at the door behind me, 'And here they are, bang on time.'

And there indeed they were. They both looked slightly alarmed by Evans's presence. 'You've got the documents?' Ryan asked.

'Sure have,' I replied.

'Good, just a moment, got one or two things to sort out' and he went to the small door with a drawing of a pair of trousers on the front.

Jenny pulled me aside, 'Shane, haven't you told him yet? He thinks I'm going with him.'

'Ssh,' I replied, 'I'll tell him just before the boat departs. That way he'll have less time to think about it. Trust me.'

'Mr Shane,' said Ryan coming out of the little boys' room, 'Can I say thank you so much for all your help.'

'Don't mention it.'

He pulled up his sleeve and displayed his wristy. It was quite a nice one actually, not one of those standard black plastic things, this one was stainless steel. 'Now I'll need your details,' he said.

'Save the money until you get to America, you'll need it over there.'

'Thank you very much,' He looked at Jenny as if he was trying to work out what was going on. 'Are you sure that's what you want?'

I put my hand inside my jacket, I said, 'Quite sure,'

and pulled out the envelope, and passed it to him. He took it and looked at it. Suspiciously for a moment, and then put it in his own jacket.

It was at that moment that Rhys Evans said, stentoriously, 'Andrew Ryan, you are under arrest, for the possession of stolen travel documents, and for the murder of the English courier who was carrying them.'

Ryan looked around first at Jenny, who edged slightly closer to me, and then at me with a look of utter loathing and contempt. 'What?' he said, 'You were both in this together?'

Rhys Evans walked towards him, holding out a pair of handcuffs. 'You're surprised at them?' he said drily, 'It appears that they thought about things in general and lust won.' He turned round and was about to thank me when he realised I was holding Jenny's revolver and it was pointing straight at him.

'Not so fast, Rhys,' I said. 'I don't think anybody's getting arrested for the moment.'

'What? Shane have you taken leave of your senses?'

'Probably, but this is the decision I have decided to take.'

'You do realise what this means for everybody don't you?'

'I imagine so, but in the meantime, those documents may not need any official stamp, but they still need validating by the police. So I'm asking you to do that. Right now.' I passed him a ballpoint from the top of the departure desk. He looked down at the gun and my hand, which was remarkably steady considering I'd never fired a gun in anger at anyone in my life.

'And what would you like me to put?'

'The names on those documents should be Mister and Mrs. Andrew Ryan.' I said.

'And that's what you want me to put?'

'That's what I want you to put.'

'And if I don't?'

'I shall put a bullet right through your heart.'

He started signing the documents, muttering, 'I can think of other places I might find more painful.' He passed the documents back to Ryan, and I called a baggage handler, and asked him to escort their bags to the boat. For a moment Ryan followed them while Evans still watched the gun I still had pointed at him.

'What?' That one came from Jenny. 'What about us? Last night we said..'

I interrupted her. 'Last night we said a great many things, not all of which were true. What is true is that right now we are sitting on a nasty little shit storm of an island that is drifting out into the middle of the Atlantic where it won't bother anybody, least of all, itself. On this island you will find corrupt officials and starving kids, and nothing else to recommend it either. Now that man,' I jerked a thumb at Ryan, 'may just have the answers to some of those problems.' While keeping a weather eye on Evans, I added, 'and that man loves you. You are the reason he gets up in the morning, and fights the battles he fights. I don't know how he does it, but I do know what might stop him, and I don't want to do that. So you're getting on that boat with him, because if you don't, you'll regret it soon, and maybe for the rest of your life.' I looked across at Rhys, 'Isn't that right Rhys?'

'I don't know,' he replied, 'it started getting soppy and I switched off.'

'Go and get that boat moving,' I said, waving him

across to the communicator on the departures desk.

He picked up the rather old fashioned desk-communicator, 'Superintendent Rhys Evans here. Those travel documents in the name of Andrew Ryan are genuine, I repeat, genuine. Prepare for departure with the tide.' He looked at me, 'how was that?' he asked.

'That should do,' I replied.

'Andrew,' I said calling out to the man at the back of the room, trying to look inconspicuous. 'Just so as you know, Jenny was round my place last night.'

'I don't have to know this,' he said.

'No. But I'd just as soon you did. She tried everything to persuade me to give up those tickets. She even tried to persuade me she was still in love with me. Me, shitty little turd that I am. I might have even led her on a bit, but she was there batting for your team the whole time. I *am* still in love with her, and my request to you is that wherever you go, whatever you do, you look after that woman as if your life depends on it. It probably did here today, and it may yet do so again.' I offered him my hand.

'Look after yourself, Shane,' he replied, 'and welcome back to the war. This time I know which is going to be the winning side.'

He put his hand on Jenny's and steered her through the gate.

§§§§

They had hardly disappeared, when there was a loud squealing of brakes outside. Somebody was driving something other than an official pod. There was a crash through the waiting room door, and Colonel Willoughby stood in front of us, obviously fuming.

When was he ever not fuming?

'What was the meaning of that?' he howled at Evans with breath that was in desperate need of assistance from a good mouthwash, which probably hadn't been available in Holyhead for a considerable period of time. 'Is Ryan on that boat going to Ireland? That must not be allowed to happen. Do something about it.'

Evans looked down at the pistol in my hand. 'I would,' he replied drily, 'but Shane has different views on the matter.

Willoughby looked down at the pistol and up to me. He walked over to the communicator on the desk. 'Hello, Is that the Captain?'

'Put it down.' I snapped, 'now.'

He looked at me, and then said into the mouthpiece, 'and you're preparing to sail on the tide?' He was drawing a pistol of his own from his webbing belt when I shot him. He looked surprised for a moment, dropped the communicator and collapsed on the floor.

The room was suddenly swarming with police.

Evans was suddenly everywhere directing traffic. 'Colonel Willoughby has just been shot,' he said. 'Round up the usual suspects.'

After a moment, he eased me through into the departure lounge. 'Come on mate,' he said, 'I really do think there are better places for you to be than here right now.'

'What do you mean?' I asked.

He put his hand into his pocket and drew out an envelope. 'I've got a couple of travel documents of my own here. I think that right now, you could really use one.' He paused. 'You know something? I'm getting pretty browned off with Holyhead too. right now; I've got all those winnings of our bet sitting in your wristy. Provided we live reasonably frugally for a while, I'm sure we can make ends meet. Why don't I come along with you for the ride?'

'Where are we going?'

'That boat is going to Dublin, and from there we can go anywhere. I'm told that Sydney can be quite a pleasant place to be at this time of the year, all that cricket and the Sydney opera house. They say there's going to be a really good cricket Tri-Series coming up. India and the Americans are going to tour Australia together.'

'You know something, watching India play the States in a Test Match would be superb. Have the Americans got that pair of Comanche quick bowlers touring with them?'

'Yes, and that mad Mohawk wicket keeper.'

'Getting better by the minute, this exile idea.'

We walked out into the drizzle and up the steps onto the ship. He waved his documents at the woman at the embarkation point, but she didn't take a lot of notice of them, just waving us to 'Go to deck six.'

'One thing,' he said, 'While we're on this boat, please give Jenny Laing a wide berth. I would hate to be a third wheel.'

'You know something, cobber,' I said. 'This may be the beginning of a beautiful relationship.'

CASABLANCA DIRECTED BY MICHAEL CURTIZ

Casablanca released in early 1943 has remained one of the most popular Hollywood films ever since. It was just one of many films made at the time, and while it was known that it had a reputable cast of good actors, and had a good crew behind it, it was not expected to do any more than entertain the masses until the next good film came along, probably within the next few weeks. In fact the makers were still faintly surprised that it was still in mind when the Oscars came along at the end of the year. They were even more surprised when it won three: Best Film, Best Director and Best Screenplay! But even those accolades don't explain its lasting popularity.

Its stars, Humphrey Bogart, Ingrid Bergman, Claude Rains, Conrad Veidt, Sydney Greenstreet, Peter Lorre, and Paul Henreid, were all popular journeyman in Hollywood at the time. Bogart, Lorre and Greenstreet were often seen in Warner Brothers films together, such as The Maltese Falcon, and Across the Pacific. They seemed to come as a package. Ingrid Bergman, a Swedish actress, was under contract to David O. Selznick, who swapped her with Warner Brothers who had Olivia de Havilland under contract, and Selznick wanted de Havilland for a picture of his own. William Wyler, the producer's first choice for director was unavailable, so Curtiz, an ex-Hungarian Jew, brought over to Hollywood as a cinematographer in the 1920s, and who spent the rest of the silent pictures period learning to speak English and making silent pictures, was selected as he wasn't doing anything in particular at the time, and with Curtiz came Claude Rains an English actor who played the Sheriff of Nottingham in Curtiz's The Adventures of Robin Hood. How Paul Henreid, an Austrian who came over in 1935, got the gig is lost in the mists of time, but he didn't get on with the rest of the cast, even Conrad Veidt, a well-known actor in Germany who escaped from the Nazis to Hollywood, and spent most of the rest of his film career playing Nazis. He wouldn't complain though, as he was the highest paid member of the cast.

The Screenplay was written in lumps by Howard Koch and the Epstein Brothers, all of whom had other [?bigger] projects they were working on at the time, and certainly when filming was started in May 1942, the script was unfinished. It was based on a play called *Everybody Comes to Rick's*, by Murray Burnett and Joan Alison. It hadn't been produced in a theatre anywhere, but it had got itself into Warner Brothers library, and Hal B. Wallis bought the rights to make the movie in 1942, The story went that according to Bergman, she was regularly asking which of the two men, Bogart or Henreid she was supposed to be in love with, she was told to play both men the same, as they weren't quite sure of the ending yet, and the original stage play was ambiguous too.

After its release it was a solid if unspectacular success. It made a profit, but at a little over a $1m cost to make, it didn't have to be an enormous hit to break even. However it became a conversation piece. There was a competition in the 1950s about the 100 most memorable lines from Hollywood Movies and Casablanca won it hands down over classics like Gone With The Wind and Citizen Kane, even after all the misquotes were cut out, like 'Play it *again* Sam' which never appeared in the picture. One of the favourite quotes was 'Here's looking at you kid' which apparently Bogart ad-libbed during a down-time card game with Bergman, and Koch who was also playing, liked it and wrote it in.

It never garners the Number 1 accolade in 'best picture of all time' lists, but in all of them it features. With its combination of wartime drama, romance, dry comedy, tension, and twists, it was probably the most generally complete picture of all, and it remains one of the most popular films ever with the man in the street. Nobody dislikes it, and if it appears on the TV, as it does often, it never gathers a 'not that old chestnut again' comment.

To describe the plot to someone who doesn't know the film would be a spoiler. Who doesn't know it anyway? It is available on Netflix or a Sky library near you. It is also available on DVD for next to nothing. Settle down and watch it. It's an hour and three quarters of sheer unadulterated pleasure.

The play, *Everyone Comes to Rick's*, has been performed in theatres occasionally since, without much success. They have talked about making a film sequel, but it never got off the ground. Someone tried to recirculate the screenplay around various production companies under the title of *Everyone Comes to Rick's* and changing Sam's name to Dooley. It was universally rejected, and only one or two people even recognised Casablanca in the script. One wag suggested that perhaps it would do better as a novel.

As a film it is living proof of the old adage that you can't create magic, it just requires all the different ingredients to crystallise and magic happens, and in

Casablanca it did so, spectacularly.

Incidentally it is my favourite picture too, from a very eclectic list, and when this idea was put to me, I couldn't resist it.

THE NOVELLA NOSTALGIA SERIES

This publishing initiative brings together the uniqueness of the novella and various memorable movies from the history of cinema.

The word 'novella' comes from the Italian for 'novel.' It has been interpreted in various ways including 'a long short story' or a 'short novel'. It can be traced back to the early renaissance in Italy and France. Giovanni Boccaccio wrote 'The Decameron' in 1353. This comprises 100 tales of ten people fleeing the black death. It was not until the 18th and 19th centuries that the novella emerged as a literary genre.

In 1941, the Austrian novelist Stefan Zweig wrote 'The Chess Novella' which was later renamed 'The Royal Game'. This was the inspiration for the 1960 film 'Brainwashed'.

Most modern novellas are published by Penguin Modern Classics. The various novella prizes seem to stipulate a word count of between 7,500 and 40,000. A key feature of the novella is its limited punctuation. There are no chapter headings and no breaks apart from spaces where the author needs to show a scene change.

Full details of the Novella Nostalgia series can be found at www.cityfiction.co.uk.

ABOUT THE AUTHOR

Richard (Dick) Cartmel is a retired General Practitioner and lives in Peterborough, United Kingdom.

He has combined his love of fine wines, politics and human nature when writing a series of six novels.

A French police officer features in three - *The Inspector Truchaud Mystery* series - which takes him into the vineyards of Burgundy.

His well-reviewed book, *North Sea Rising*, envisages a post-Brexit Britain in 2039.

Dick Cartmel cleverly picks up this theme in his novella *The White House: Holyhead*. This is his first publication for City Fiction Limited.

Full details and contact can be found on:

Email   dick.cartmel@gmail.com
WWW   rmcartmelauthor.com
Twitter   @cartmelDr